Even _ _ She watched. _____ saw a _reak of lightning split th_ _____ _ _____

"Sto___" she ____ "_____ _____ _ons over the At-lantic. I_ ____ ____ _____ ___ _____, then the American Airways flight from New York could have been, too. It wouldn't have arrived until *ten*-fifteen! Which means . . ."

"Moore . . ."

"Clark . . ."

"He *could* have been on it!"

She checked her watch. Just enough time. She turned back toward the computer room.

"Where are you going?" called Josh.

"To e-mail Tom. We need a picture of that guy!"

INTERNET DETECTIVES

ELECTRONIC MAIL

File   Edit   View   Options   Window   Utilities   Favelist   Help

From: Sent:
To: Subject:

michael coleman
ESCAPE KEY

OPEN   SEND   FORWARD   REPLY   DELETE   SAVE   PRINT

Mail:

A SKYLARK BOOK

NEW YORK • TORONTO • LONDON • SYDNEY • AUCKLAND

For Brian Bloor, with many thanks

RL 4, 008–012

ESCAPE KEY

A Bantam Skylark Book/October 1997

Skylark Books is a registered trademark of Bantam Books, a division of Bantam Doubleday Dell Publishing Group, Inc. Registered in U.S. Patent and Trademark Office and elsewhere.

First published 1996 by Macmillan Children's Books, a division of Macmillan Publishers Limited.

Created by Working Partners Limited
London W6 0HE

ISBN 0-553-48621-7

PRINTED IN THE UNITED STATES OF AMERICA

OPM 0 9 8 7 6 5 4 3 2 1

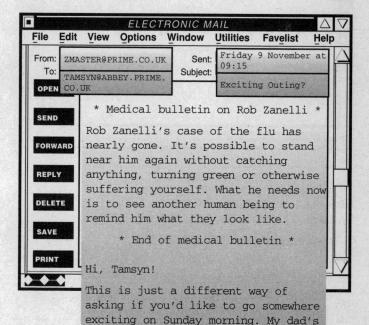

CHAPTER 1

ELECTRONIC MAIL

File   Edit   View   Options   Window   Utilities   Favelist   Help

From: ZMASTER@PRIME.CO.UK
To: TAMSYN@ABBEY.PRIME.CO.UK

Sent: Friday 9 November at 09:15
Subject: Exciting Outing?

OPEN

SEND

FORWARD

REPLY

DELETE

SAVE

PRINT

* Medical bulletin on Rob Zanelli *

Rob Zanelli's case of the flu has nearly gone. It's possible to stand near him again without catching anything, turning green or otherwise suffering yourself. What he needs now is to see another human being to remind him what they look like.

     * End of medical bulletin *

Hi, Tamsyn!

This is just a different way of asking if you'd like to go somewhere exciting on Sunday morning. My dad's due back from his trip to San Francisco and I'm going with Mom to meet him at Heathrow Airport. Wanna come too?

Rob

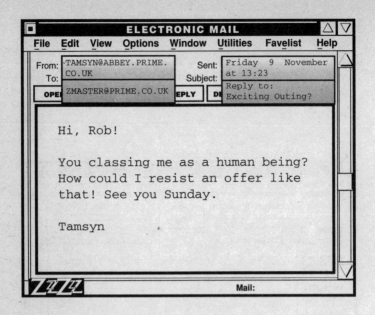

Heathrow Airport, London
Sunday, November 11, 10:20 A.M.

"Oh no!" groaned Rob.

As Tamsyn Smith looked his way, Rob pointed up at the square monitor suspended from the ceiling.

ARRIVALS			
10:25	AA46	SAN FRANCISCO	DELAYED

Moments later, a voice over the airport loudspeaker confirmed what the display had just told them.

"American Airways flight forty-six from San Francisco will be approximately one hour late in arriving. This is due to adverse weather conditions over the Atlantic Ocean."

"They should have used the Internet to check it out before they left," said Rob. "It's got plenty of weather reports!"

Sitting opposite the two friends, Mrs. Zanelli laughed. Her son's fascination with computers was no surprise. Both she and Mr. Zanelli owned and ran a successful computer software company, which was why Rob's father had been in America. Hardly a day went by without Rob's telling them about something new he'd found on the Internet, the worldwide network of computers.

"Even the Internet can't keep up with the weather sometimes," said Mrs. Zanelli. She looked around at the bustling crowds. "Look, I'm going for a cup of coffee. Would you two like another drink?"

"No, thank you, Mrs. Zanelli," said Tamsyn. "I'm fine." Rob's mother had been buying them drinks and candy ever since they'd arrived.

"You go, Mom," said Rob. "We'll be okay here."

"Are you sure?" Mrs. Zanelli said doubtfully.

Rob swung his wheelchair around. "Completely sure! Tamsyn here will lie down in front of me if it looks like I'm rolling away!"

"Well . . ." Mrs. Zanelli paused, then finally headed off across the airport concourse.

Rob shook his head as she went. His parents were both very protective of him, and he understood why.

Rob had lost the use of his legs in a car accident when he was eight, and although it hadn't been their fault in any way, it had left them feeling frightened to let Rob out of their sight.

For a long while he hadn't been allowed to go to a normal school. He'd always had tutors come in to teach him at home—until one of his tutors joined forces with a crook to try to steal a valuable computer disk from his father's study! That escapade, which Rob, Tamsyn, and their friend Josh Allan had foiled, had shown his parents that he wasn't completely helpless. They'd finally agreed that he could go to Abbey School with Tamsyn and Josh.

"So, what are we going to do?" Rob asked Tamsyn. "It looks like we've got some time to kill."

"Well, I'm all right," said Tamsyn, fishing in her book bag and bringing out a book. "I brought my English homework with me."

"You're not going to sit there and read *Oliver Twist!*" said Rob. "You sneak! You'll be a hundred pages in front of the rest of us by tomorrow's class."

"You mean you haven't brought your book?" laughed Tamsyn.

"How can I? I'm reading the version on the Internet!" Rob shook his head. "If Dad makes me wait around airports too often, I may just have to ask him to get me a portable PC!"

Tamsyn closed her book. "All right, I won't read. But what are we going to do—play I Spy?"

Rob brightened. "Now you're talking!"

Tamsyn gave him a horrified look. "I was only joking! I haven't played that for years!"

"Ah, I wasn't talking about *that* sort of I Spy," said Rob. "I was talking about *my* version of I Spy. It's different. What you do is pick somebody out of the crowd and imagine where they've come from"—his voice grew low and creepy as he looked around at the mass of people—"and what they've been doing! Her, for instance," said Rob, pointing at a woman on the far side of the concourse.

Tamsyn looked over at the woman. She was well dressed and had a pair of sunglasses perched on top of her head. Just ahead of her, a rather battered-looking man was trying to push a luggage cart piled high with suitcases.

"A movie star," said Tamsyn, immediately getting the idea of the game.

"Is that why she's wearing sunglasses?"

"No, she's forgotten she's got them on," said Tamsyn. "Because she's just flown in from somewhere hot and exotic, like . . . Tahiti! That's where she's been making her latest movie." She turned to Rob. "What do you think?"

Rob shook his head. "Not very imaginative, Smith."

Tamsyn ran a hand through her short dark hair, her eyes glinting. "All right, Mr. Clever. What's *your* suggestion?"

"A suitcase smuggler," said Rob. "Those are all unbelievably expensive suitcases and she's paying that guy to push that cart for her. Those suitcases are empty."

"It doesn't look like it," remarked Tamsyn with a laugh as the man pushing the cart stopped to mop his brow.

"Okay," said Rob. "They're not empty. They're . . . yes, they're full of other suitcases. Smaller ones, all nested like Russian dolls!"

Tamsyn giggled, then looked around. At the far end of their row of seats a man had just gotten to his feet. "Okay, then," she said. "How about him?"

"Airport bum," said Rob at once. "Out for an afternoon stroll."

The man Tamsyn had pointed out was wearing a very creased, pale-colored suit. His tie was hanging loose, and his collar was open. The man's short dark hair didn't look as though it had been combed. As he took off his glasses and looked up at a nearby airport directory, Tamsyn noticed something glint in the light.

"A bum?" she whispered. "With a diamond stud in his ear?"

"A rich bum," replied Rob. "Yes, that's it. Look at those bags."

The man was holding two bags, one a flight bag with an American Airways logo on the side, the other a shopping bag from one of the most expensive stores at the airport.

"Dad often buys Mom some perfume from that place," said Rob. "And he always tells her how much it cost him!"

Tamsyn laughed. "So what's he doing with it? What's he doing here?"

Rob rubbed his chin in mock thoughtfulness. "That bag contains all he owns in the world. Because he's a rich and nutty international bum who spends all his money jetting around the world and sleeping on seats in different airports!"

Over by the directory the man seemed to have found what he was looking for. He moved off again.

"So where's he going now?" wondered Tamsyn. "Back to the five-star seat he's selected for tonight?"

"Er . . . no," said Rob, suddenly realizing why the scruffy man had been looking at the directory. "He's on his way to the men's room!"

As the man disappeared, Tamsyn and Rob turned their attention to other unsuspecting travelers. They'd been playing the game for more than ten minutes when Rob noticed the man emerging from the men's room again.

"Hey—isn't that Mr. Scruffy?"

"Is it?" said Tamsyn, looking hard.

The man coming their way bore little resemblance to the one who'd gone in. The crumpled suit had been replaced by a pressed jacket and trousers. His collar and tie were now neatly arranged. His hair was swept back and tidy.

"Certainly is," said Rob, pointing. "Diamond stud in his left ear, see?"

The two friends sat and stared, their game forgotten.

The man was turning from side to side, as if looking for something again.

Suddenly he moved. Tamsyn felt her nerves stretch as he walked toward them. Had he seen them looking at him and laughing? Tamsyn tried to turn away and keep her eye on him at the same time. He was still coming! Closer . . . closer . . .

As he stopped just a couple of feet away from them, Tamsyn barely managed to suppress a little squeak of relief. He hadn't been heading for them at all—he was walking toward the big trash can at the end of the row of seats.

Tamsyn and Rob exchanged a silent glance as the man reached the trash. They saw him pause as he realized that it was almost overflowing with garbage. Then, in one sharp movement, he stuffed his shopping bag on top anyway and strode quickly away.

"Phew!" said Tamsyn. "I thought he was coming for us!"

Rob laughed. "Hey, your imagination *is* improving!" He nodded in the direction of the trash can. "Come on, then. I Spy version two. What did he put in there?"

"Huh?"

"The garbage. What do you think Mr. Diamond Earring has thrown away? And don't tell me all his money!"

Tamsyn brushed her hair back. "Pretty obvious, isn't it? That dirty old crumpled suit he was wearing."

Rob's eyes narrowed. "Ah, but why? Do you think it's a plant?"

"No, I just told you," said Tamsyn with a glint in her eye. "I think it's a suit."

"You know what I mean!" said Rob. "A drop. He could be a spy, and any minute now his contact will be coming along to fish that suit out of there because its pockets are full of top-secret—"

"What?" asked Tamsyn. "Top-secret lint?"

"Ah," said Rob, "but it might not be real lint. It could be fake lint, actually made up of microdots!"

Tamsyn couldn't resist. She looked around again. The man had disappeared into the crowd of people hurrying around the airport. She edged along the bench toward the trash can.

"There's only one way to find out," she said.

Reaching one hand gingerly into the trash, Tamsyn pulled the top of the shopping bag to one side. Sure enough, the pale material of the crumpled suit was in there.

"There you go," said Rob. "Now check the pockets for microdots."

Tamsyn wrinkled her nose. "No way!" she cried.

Rob edged close and peered into the shopping bag. The man had obviously stuffed the trousers into it first, and the jacket second. Rob could see the soiled edge of its collar. He opened the bag a little further. Now he could see the trim of the jacket's breast pocket. A small triangle of white card was peeping out from it.

"Rob! What are you doing?"

Rob had put his hand into the trash and inserted a finger into the breast pocket.

"A business card," he said, pulling it out.

CHEC**K**R**M**A**N**ATE
Multimedia Training Systems

Kelvin B. Moore
President

78 Queensbury Street, Perth, Australia
e-mail: topman@check.co.au

"Clearly not an international bum after all," said Rob. "An international big shot instead."

"That's it," said Tamsyn. "He was traveling in an international-bum disguise! And a very good one it was, too! You had us fooled," she said to the suit, poking her finger into the shopping bag as she did so.

As the bag moved, a flimsy slip of paper fell out. Tamsyn picked it up.

"What is it?" said Rob, seeing Tamsyn frown.

"A credit card receipt. For nearly five hundred dollars."

Rob moved his wheelchair away from the trash can and edged back toward Tamsyn. "For his new gear, I suppose."

Tamsyn nodded. It wasn't possible to tell. The box on the credit card receipt simply read "merchandise."

"Kelvin B. Moore, eccentric millionaire," said Rob.

"Who?" said Mrs. Zanelli, returning from the coffee shop.

Rob laughed. "Nothing, Mom. Just a game we were playing."

As Tamsyn saw that Mrs. Zanelli had brought with

her yet another tray full of drinks and cookies, she tucked both the business card and the credit card slip inside her copy of *Oliver Twist*.

And so it wasn't until that evening, when she opened it again, that she noticed that the signature at the bottom of the credit card slip wasn't that of Kelvin B. Moore at all, but of somebody completely different.

K. M. Clark

CHAPTER 2

Toronto, Canada
Sunday, November 11, 8:55 P.M.

"Lauren, what are you doing? This room looks like it's hosting a chess tournament!"

Lauren King turned to her grandmother. Alice—or Allie, as Lauren had always called her—was standing in the doorway, a dinner tray in her hands.

"It *is* a chess tournament, Allie. Kind of."

"Well, I would call it a kind of something, too," said Alice. "A kind of mess!"

She marched into the room, looking from side to side. "Now, where can I put this tray? You know, I used to have a dining table in here somewhere, I swear I did."

Lauren sighed. Carefully she eased aside one of the five chess sets she'd laid out on the table. Alice plunked the tray down in the gap.

"Lauren," said Alice, "either this stuff goes, or you do!"

"I don't think you mean that, Allie," said Lauren.

But, just to be sure, she looked into her grand-mother's eyes. Lauren had lived with Alice ever since her own parents had been drowned in a boating accident, and she'd learned what to look for. It was okay—Alice's eyes were twinkling.

"Maybe I don't," said Alice. "But I could sure do with a bigger apartment sometimes! How many games have you got going at once now?"

"Five," said Lauren. "I'm playing Josh over the Internet. We e-mail each other our next moves."

"Josh and who else?"

"Nobody. Just Josh."

"Five games at once?" exclaimed Alice.

Lauren nodded. "I know. But it's his fault. Every time it looks like I'm ahead, he wants to start another game!"

Alice sprinkled some salt on a stick of celery. "Well, I hope you're going to win one soon," she said, depositing the salt shaker on one of the chessboards, "or there'll be no room to move in here!"

"I think I'm about to, Allie," said Lauren, removing the salt shaker, "even if you are giving Josh extra pieces!"

She studied the board thoughtfully. Her previous few moves in this game had put her into a good attack position. Now . . . Lauren smiled as she saw the move she had to make. "Got him!" she said.

Alice looked up as Lauren went across the room and turned on the computer sitting in the corner. "Not at this time of night . . ."

"Allie, please! I want to make sure Josh gets this first thing tomorrow. I've got him in checkmate!"

Alice relented. "Oh, all right. If it gets one of these boards off my table, then it's worth it. But that's all. No sailing the Net tonight."

"*Surfing*, Allie. How many times have I told you? It's called surfing the Net."

"Surfing, sailing," said Alice. "You send that one note and then it's bed. Got me?"

Lauren looked into her grandmother's eyes. No twinkle. "Got you, Allie." She nodded solemnly.

Toronto, Canada
9:50 P.M.

Alice peered around the door of her granddaughter's room. Seeing the sleeping figure, she smiled quietly to herself. At last!

She returned to the living room. In the corner, their computer was still on, its display glowing. It had been an expensive purchase, but Lauren gained so much from using it.

And not only Lauren. Alice sat down and adjusted her glasses. Her fingers reached out toward the mouse and clicked on the globe icon. Within moments she was connected to the Internet.

"Time for a little sailing," she chuckled.

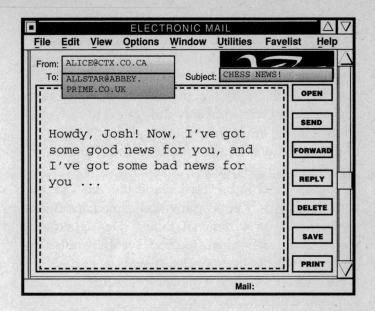

ELECTRONIC MAIL

File   Edit   View   Options   Window   Utilities   Favelist   Help

From: ALICE@CTX.CO.CA
To: ALLSTAR@ABBEY.
PRIME.CO.UK

Subject: CHESS NEWS!

Howdy, Josh! Now, I've got
some good news for you, and
I've got some bad news for
you ...

OPEN

SEND

FORWARD

REPLY

DELETE

SAVE

PRINT

Mail:

Abbey School, Portsmouth
Monday, November 12, 8:30 A.M.

Tamsyn mentioned the signature on the bottom of the credit card slip when she met Rob in the school's technology wing the next day.

"Of course, the explanation is simple," she added.

"It is?" said Rob.

"Yes. The guy's name was Clark, same as on the credit card receipt. He came in on some long-distance flight and decided he'd lived in his clothes for long enough and couldn't stand the sight of them anymore."

"That I can believe," said Rob. "I didn't like the look of them and they weren't even mine!"

"So he buys a whole new outfit the moment he steps off the plane and throws his old stuff in the trash."

"And the Kelvin B. Moore card?" asked Rob, wheeling to a halt outside a door marked Computer Club.

"Given to Clark by Moore himself. That's the obvious part. They were probably sitting next to each other on the plane. One of them mentioned his PC, they got to talking, and the next thing you know they're exchanging business cards."

"Right," said Rob. "Businesspeople are like that with their cards. I've seen my dad come back from a conference with dozens of them." He sighed. "So there's no mystery, then. Too bad. I really wanted another case for the Internet Detectives."

He opened the door. Following him through, Tamsyn looked around the room.

"Now here's a mystery for you," she said.

"What?"

"A computer room without Josh!" she said, gesturing toward the computer in the far corner of the room.

Rob cottoned on at once. "You're right," he said. "A Josh-less computer room? Call the police! Something awful must have happened to him!"

Suddenly a low groaning sound came from the corner of the room. "Something awful *has* happened to me."

Slowly a thatch of spiky, uncontrollable hair slid into view, followed closely by a face wearing a look of total misery. "Come and see for yourself."

Rob eased his wheelchair around to where Josh was sitting. Tamsyn stood behind them—and saw why Josh had been bent low behind his computer. In front of him was a portable chess set, its pieces set out as though in the middle of a game. Alongside it was a scruffy notepad, its pages covered in notes of chess moves.

And on the screen was the e-mail that Lauren had sent the night before:

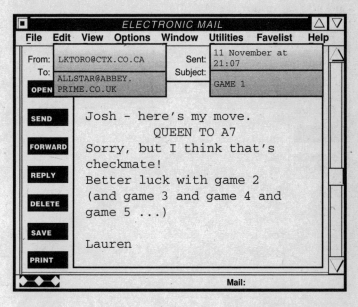

Rob studied the board briefly. Josh's king was hemmed in on all sides. "I think that's checkmate, too," he said.

"Losing is bad enough," groaned Josh. "But—"

"I know, Josh," mocked Tamsyn, "but losing to a *girl* . . ."

Josh riffled the pages of his notebook. "And I've got another four games going in here!"

Snapping the chess set shut, he reached out and slid the computer's mouse sideways until the arrow-shaped cursor was poised over the Delete icon. One sharp click, and the e-mail had been erased.

At the bottom of the screen, the line Mail: 1 Message Waiting was flashing. Josh checked it out. "Hey," he said. "It's a note from Alice."

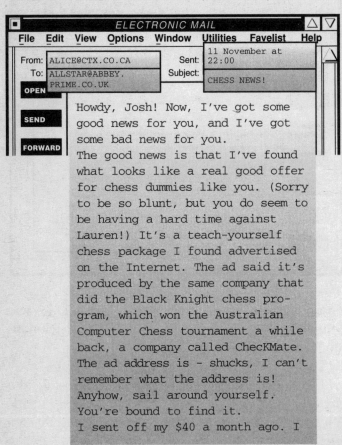

ELECTRONIC MAIL

File   Edit   View   Options   Window   Utilities   Favelist   Help

From: ALICE@CTX.CO.CA   Sent: 11 November at 22:00
To: ALLSTAR@ABBEY.   Subject:
      PRIME.CO.UK   CHESS NEWS!

OPEN

SEND

FORWARD

Howdy, Josh! Now, I've got some good news for you, and I've got some bad news for you.
The good news is that I've found what looks like a real good offer for chess dummies like you. (Sorry to be so blunt, but you do seem to be having a hard time against Lauren!) It's a teach-yourself chess package I found advertised on the Internet. The ad said it's produced by the same company that did the Black Knight chess pro-gram, which won the Australian Computer Chess tournament a while back, a company called ChecKMate. The ad address is - shucks, I can't remember what the address is! Anyhow, sail around yourself. You're bound to find it.
I sent off my $40 a month ago. I

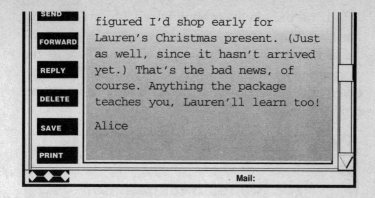

figured I'd shop early for
Lauren's Christmas present. (Just
as well, since it hasn't arrived
yet.) That's the bad news, of
course. Anything the package
teaches you, Lauren'll learn too!

Alice

Mail:

"Is that a coincidence, or is that a coincidence?" said Tamsyn. She was already rummaging in her book bag.

"That is a coincidence," said Rob.

Josh frowned at his two friends. "Huh?"

"ChecKMate," said Tamsyn. She'd opened her copy of *Oliver Twist* and pulled out the business card. "We found this at Heathrow Airport yesterday. It was in the pocket of a jacket somebody threw away."

She and Rob explained to Josh what had happened, and what they thought.

"Weird," said Josh. "But I guess you're right. Clark, whoever he was, must have met this guy Moore on the plane." His eyes lit up. "Hey, why didn't you hunt around in the old suit longer? You might have found one of those CD-ROMs he sells. I'd have been ahead of Lauren for once!"

Tamsyn moved to another of the computers in the room and turned it on. "How about seeing if we can find the ad Alice was talking about?"

Rob did the same, settling himself in front of a third machine. "Good idea. Bet I find it first."

He waited for the system to boot up. Then, as the opening page of choices was displayed, he clicked on one marked Newsgroups. Moments later he was scanning a long list:

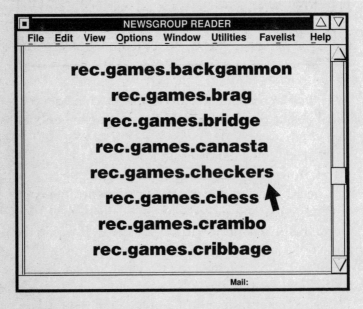

Rob knew there was a vast number of newsgroups on the Internet—electronic bulletin boards to which people the world over posted information. They covered just about every topic under the sun. So, he figured, it was likely that there was a chess newsgroup.

He scanned the list. Yes, there it was. He moved to the line reading and double-clicked.

This sent him into the middle of a pile of notes. Just like e-mail messages, they'd been posted to the newsgroup for all to read. If Alice couldn't remember where on the Net she'd seen her chess ad, maybe there'd be a newsgroup note to tell him.

He looked through a few about opening move strategies. Then he found one.

> Anybody else out there respond to the Check-
> Mate CD-ROM ad of a few weeks back? I did, and
> I'm still waiting for mine to show.

Rob clicked on the Next button in the toolbar. Another message was asking the same thing.

> I'd like to hear from anybody who's received
> the CheckMate CD-ROM. My check was cashed
> pretty fast, but the company doesn't seem so
> quick at sending out their product.

A couple of notes later, there was a third.

> There was a Chess Tutor CD-ROM advertised on
> the Net a while back. I made a note of the
> URL:
>   http://www.check.co.au
> Anybody else send off their $40 for this? I
> did, and I think it could be the last I see of
> it. The mailman's brought me nothing. Not only
> that, but I can't find the ad anymore. Am I
> the only one who's been ripped off here?

Rob whistled. "Come and look at these," he said.

"Not so good," said Josh after he'd read the messages. "This ChecKMate company sounds pretty disreputable."

"Maybe it's a crooked company," said Tamsyn. She tapped the business card, still on the desk beside Rob's keyboard. "Maybe our rumpled Mr. Clark met the one and only Kelvin Moore—and was the last person to see him! Maybe Moore is a man on the run!"

Rob and Josh exchanged glances. "Or maybe that guy *was* Moore," said Rob.

Josh laughed. "Yeah, he met this guy Clark on the plane, ripped off his credit card, then shoved him out of the emergency exit while the flight attendant wasn't looking! Come on, Tamsyn. Save the imagination for English class. This is real life."

"Okay, okay," said Tamsyn with a smile. But she was already sliding back onto her chair. "Forget the man-on-the-run idea."

"So what are you up to?" asked Rob.

"Just sending a few notes around," said Tamsyn. "There's no point having a team of Internet Detectives and not giving them any Internet detecting to do! And we have got a player on the scene, don't we?"

"Tom?"

"Who else? He lives in Perth—and that's where this ChecKMate company is based, isn't it?"

"Right," said Rob. "Hey, copy it to Mitch as well. He'll want to know what's going on." Mitch Zanelli lived in New York. He and Rob were still trying to discover if they were related.

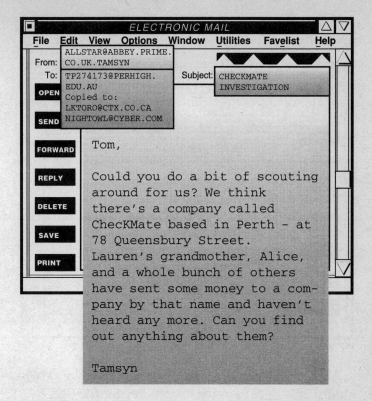

While Tamsyn typed, Rob and Josh held a whispered conversation. As Tamsyn looked quizzically at him, Rob grinned.

"What are you two up to?" she asked, sending her e-mail on its way.

Josh shrugged. "We don't see why we shouldn't go straight to the top."

Tamsyn frowned. "What do you mean, to the top?"

Rob picked up the business card and waved it.

"Like, to the president kind of top," he said. He held it up for Josh to read as he typed:

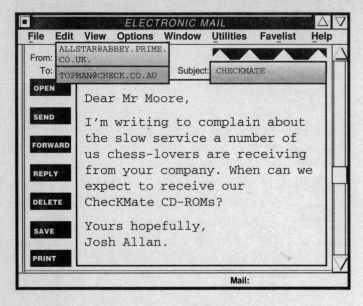

As he clicked on Send, the school bell sounded loudly outside. The three friends began to move.

"Do you think we'll get any answers by lunchtime?" Tamsyn asked.

"Not from K. B. Moore, we won't," snorted Josh. "It doesn't sound like he's in the country anyway."

"They have secretaries to do all that sort of stuff for them," said Tamsyn. "Anyway, I was thinking more of Tom."

"Ah, he's a better bet," said Josh. "What time is it in western Australia? About five o'clock in the afternoon?"

Tamsyn thought for a moment, then nodded. In Perth, where Tom lived, the time was eight hours ahead of them. It was hard to believe that Tom had already finished his school day just as they were starting theirs.

"If he's got any sense, he'll be in his backyard, lazing in a hammock with a cool drink in his hand—not sitting in front of a computer!" She looked wistfully out of the window at the gray clouds and steady drizzle. "It is *summer* in Australia, you know."

"Really, Tamsyn," said Rob, shaking his head. "For a true Internet Detective, the time of year doesn't matter." He pushed his way toward the door. "You know, I bet Tom's reading our e-mail right now. . . ."

CHAPTER 3

Perth, Australia
Monday, November 12, 5:10 P.M.

Tom Peterson wasn't lazing in the backyard, although that had been his plan. But a sudden torrential downpour just as school let out for the day had changed his mind. He'd decided to spend a couple of hours Net surfing, then laze later.

"ChecKMate?" he murmured as he read Tamsyn's note. "Never heard of them."

He jotted down the address. Queensbury Street—that was a major road in the central business district of the city. And not too far away—a Transperth bus would take him almost to the door.

Tom checked his watch. Tricky. He'd said he would be home by five-thirty at the latest. A quick phone call was needed.

Five minutes later he was putting a coin into the pay phone in the school lobby.

"Hello," came his mother's voice.

"Hi. It's me," said Tom. "Look, Mom . . . uh . . . I've

got some work to do. A real big project. I thought I'd try and check out some facts on the Internet. That okay with you?"

He waited for the blast. "And when are you going to clean out the garage? You promised you'd do it today. There's so much junk in there, I'm scared I'll find a pack of rats underneath it all. If your father sees it—"

"Mom," interrupted Tom. "Tomorrow, okay? I promise."

Mrs. Peterson sighed. "Tomorrow."

Tom was just about to hang up when a sudden thought occurred to him. "Um . . . Dad won't see it before then?"

"No," said Tom's mother. "He called a little while ago. He's out on a case. Won't be in till late."

With a sigh of relief, Tom hung up. He could usually figure out a way to get around his mom, but his dad was a different matter. A detective in the Perth police force, he could see through an excuse as though it was made of glass!

It took about twenty minutes on the bus before Tom saw the sign for Queensbury Street. He walked along, looking for number 78.

He stopped as he saw it. Number 78 was a set of double glass doors, fronting a small vestibule. Apart from an overgrown potted plant, there was nothing more to see than a set of stairs.

Pushing open one door, Tom stepped hesitantly inside. From above, there came voices and sounds of movement. Should he go up? Why not? It was just a business, wasn't it? The stairs probably led to a posh office, humming with life.

Tom began to make his way up the stairs. He pulled the collar of his school blazer close to his neck, imagining he was a real detective heading up to confront a suspect. The stairs ended on a small square landing. Ahead of him was a door with the name Kelvin B. Moore, Inc. emblazoned on the frosted glass.

Through the glass he could make out a number of figures moving about purposefully.

He reached for the handle—and gasped as the door was opened by a man he recognized.

"Tom!"

"Uh . . . ," mumbled Tom, "hi, Dad!"

Abbey School
1:05 P.M.

"Do you want to check the e-mail?" Rob asked at lunchtime.

Tamsyn wrinkled her nose. It was warm in the library. She was curled up with a good book on a soft seat. Outside the wind was howling. For the half hour remaining before classes started again, she didn't want to go anywhere, least of all on a trek across to the computer lab.

"Not right now," she said. "Try me after school."

"How about you, Josh?" said Rob.

Josh shook his head. "Not me. Lauren might have sorted out her next move." His brow creased as he looked down at the pocket chess set in his hand. "And I need more time. Like a year or two."

Rob slipped the brake off his wheelchair. "Looks like it's me, then, guys."

Tamsyn pointed out of the window. "Rob, it's gusting like crazy out there. You'll be blown away before you reach the computer lab."

"You might even end up on the highway." Josh grinned. "And on the evening news. 'Boy in wheelchair stopped for speeding'!"

Rob laughed. He hated having to spend his life in a wheelchair, but even more he hated being treated like a freak. When Josh and Tamsyn joked with him, as they did with each other, he really enjoyed it.

Now it was his turn to put one over on them. Easing his chair between the library seats, he went over to where the school librarian was sitting. Tamsyn and Josh saw her talk to Rob, then nod. Moments later she was turning on the library's computer.

"This was connected to the Internet last week!" mouthed Rob.

Tamsyn forgot her book. Josh abandoned his chess game. Together, they moved to sit beside Rob.

There was only one message waiting. It was for Josh—and from a source they'd never come across before. The message was short and to the point.

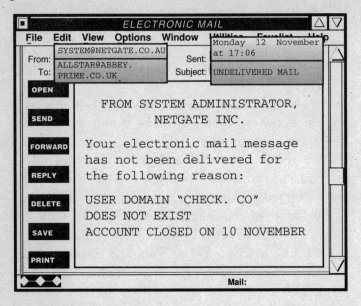

"What does that mean?" asked Josh.

Tamsyn said, "It means your mail message to Kelvin Moore hasn't gotten through."

Josh shrugged. "There you go. That's a president for you. Too busy to answer his letters."

Rob glanced at him. "Not too busy, Josh. Look at what it says. ' "CHECK.CO" does not exist.' It looks like that company isn't on the Net anymore."

Tom lay on his bed in the middle of the room he'd been made to clean as well as the garage, and fumed.

Grounded! There he was, with some red-hot information to fire across the Net to the others, and there was no way he could get onto the system until tomorrow at the earliest!

He thought back over what had happened that afternoon.

Meeting his dad at the offices of ChecKMate had been a shock, all right. But what he'd seen as he'd looked past him and into the offices of ChecKMate had shocked him even more.

The place was in chaos. Drawers and filing cabinets were open everywhere. A group of men in shirtsleeves were loading files and papers into large square boxes under the eagle eye of a uniformed police officer. Another detective, one Tom remembered as having come to their house occasionally, was talking to somebody on the telephone and jotting down details in his notebook.

Mr. Peterson had to ask his question twice before Tom realized he was being spoken to.

"Tom! I said, what are you doing here?"

Tom came straight out and told him about the e-mail he'd had from Tamsyn. "So I took the bus out here to see if I could find out more about this ChecKMate company."

"Does your mother know?"

"I called her," Tom said truthfully before quickly changing the subject. "Dad, what's going on?"

"Tax problems," said Mr. Peterson. He pointed to the men, now beginning to unload the contents of a second filing cabinet. "Those men are tax inspectors. Apparently they found a lot wrong with the company's accounts and were supposed to come in this morning to interview the boss of the outfit."

"Kelvin Moore?" asked Tom.

Mr. Peterson's eyebrows shot up. "How did you know that?"

"Tamsyn mentioned him in her e-mail," said Tom.

Again he looked around. Something didn't add up. Detectives weren't called in on tax matters. "But what are *you* doing here, Dad? Has this Moore guy been arrested?"

Mr. Peterson shook his head. "He will be when we find him. That's what we're doing here. The place was locked up, and there was no sign of this Kelvin Moore. Looks like he just dropped everything and ran."

Behind him, the second detective had finished his phone conversation. Making a final note on his pad, he stood up and walked toward them.

"What've you got, Carl?" said Mr. Peterson.

The detective glanced at Tom, giving him a quick nod of recognition. Then he said, "Looks like he's skipped the country, Pete. I just got hold of the airline people. Moore was on a flight that left Australia three days ago."

"Where to?"

"New York via Los Angeles. Landed at Kennedy Airport."

"Is he still in New York?"

"As far as we know. I hung on while they checked out the passenger lists for every flight out of Kennedy since then. Nobody by the name of Kelvin B. Moore has been on one."

"While you waited they checked out *every* flight?" Mr. Peterson said incredulously.

Tom couldn't resist. "Power of computers, Dad!"

"Okay. What else do we know?"

Carl leafed through his notebook. "Nothing for sure. Not until the tax people have gotten through all that stuff," he said with a gesture as a couple of the men struggled past them and headed off down the stairs with a paper-laden box. "But I'm betting that they'll find plenty."

Mr. Peterson looked at his colleague. "You sound pretty sure, Carl."

Carl nodded. "There was a stack of letters in a garbage bag out back, for a start. Most of them are from people asking where their money's gone, and what's happened to the things they sent for."

"Chess teaching programs?" said Tom.

"And other chess stuff," said Mr. Peterson. "Looks to me as if he got in over his head."

"What do you mean?"

Mr. Peterson glanced at his colleague. Carl began, "Moore used to be a top chess player—Australian junior champion when he was a kid. Then he discovered PCs and gave up playing to try to turn out a champion chess program. And he did—a thing called Black Knight. Apparently it won the Australian Computer Chess Tournament a couple of years ago."

Mr. Peterson took up the story. "So what does Moore do? He gets carried away. He tries to expand his business into the United States and Europe, at the same time pouring money into trying to make this Black Knight program a world-beater."

"Suddenly," said Carl, "he finds himself in trouble."

"What sort of trouble?" asked Tom.

"Out-of-money sort of trouble," Mr. Peterson said grimly. "He finds he can't pay his taxes. So he's desperate. In the end he's advertising products—like your chess tutor program—that don't even exist yet, just so he can rake in some money to pay his bills. But things only get worse. In the end he can't see a way out, so he runs."

Tom stood to one side as another overflowing box was carried out of the office and down the stairs.

"So what about the money people sent in? People like Alice?"

"Probably spent already. Either that, or Moore's stashed it in a bank account somewhere so that he can get at it later." Mr. Peterson shook his head. "Either way, she can say good-bye to it." He put his hands on Tom's shoulders. "Which is just what I'm gonna do to you. Home!"

Tom looked into the offices again. The scene of a

crime! It all looked so exciting. "Dad," he pleaded, "can't I stay?"

"Not a chance," said Mr. Peterson. "Now, home. Tell your mother I'll be another couple of hours."

Turning away, Tom trudged down the stairs to the small lobby. Through the double glass doors he could see a large van moving off into the busy traffic. *The evidence,* Tom realized as he noticed the shirtsleeved passenger and driver. All those boxes of files and papers being taken away for detailed examination.

He looked back up the stairs. A *real* criminal investigation! Too bad he wasn't allowed to see more. Irritably he pulled open the glass door, swinging it back so hard that it banged against the large potted plant. Tom anxiously threw out a hand, afraid that the plant might topple over.

That was when he saw it—a single sheet of company letterhead, wedged behind the pot.

CHECKMATE
Multimedia Training Systems

78 Queensbury Street,
Perth, Australia.
e-mail: topman@check.co.au

The rest of the page was virtually blank. *Probably a standard sheet, all ready to be loaded by the dozen into a laser printer,* thought Tom. That would account for the only other lettering on the page: Kelvin Moore's name and signature.

Kelvin B. Moore, President

All a secretary had to do was word-process a letter, then print off as many as necessary onto sheets like this. No need for the big boss to sign them at all.

Tom toyed with the paper. Should he take it back upstairs? It could be evidence. Unlikely, he decided. A sheet of letterhead? They'd have hundreds of them in those boxes already. They wouldn't miss another one—and he'd have a souvenir of a *real* investigation!

Tucking the sheet into his backpack, he swung open the door and headed for home . . .

. . . and trouble. He'd been unable to avoid passing on his dad's message about being home in a couple of hours, of course—and that had blown a hole the size of Perth Harbor in his story about staying late at school. His mother had reacted predictably.

"Then you can clean out the garage tonight! And then you can go do your room! And don't come down again until the morning!"

And that's what he'd been doing for the past three hours. Until now. Tom looked at his bedside clock.

Half past nine. Half past one in the afternoon in England.

Downstairs, his mother would be getting ready to leave the house for her part-time school-cleaning job. He leaped to his feet—then flopped back onto his bed again. Asking if he could go with her to send an e-mail from the school's computer would be pushing his luck. No, it would have to wait until tomorrow. Too bad. Still, if he sent it from school at lunchtime, they would see it first thing.

Instead, he opened one of his dresser drawers and pulled out the sheet of letterhead from beneath a pile of socks. He lay on his bed and looked at it for the umpteenth time. *A real piece of criminal memorabilia! Wait until I send the others a copy of this over the Net!*

CHAPTER 4

Manor House, Portsmouth
Tuesday, November 13, 7:30 A.M.

Rob was the first to see Tom's e-mail. He'd gotten up at his usual time of seven o'clock, slipped out of bed and into his wheels, then headed off down the corridor to the kitchen to make himself some break-fast.

His home, perched on top of Portsdown Hill over-looking Portsmouth, was old and large. Rob's room was on the ground floor, meaning that he could roam around at any time without disturbing his parents up-stairs. In the days before he'd been allowed to go to Abbey School, Rob had been irritated by Mr. and Mrs. Zanelli's determination to do absolutely everything for him. He'd gotten into the habit of getting up early and fixing his own breakfast just to prove to them that he could do it. The habit had stuck.

With a full bowl of cereal and a glass of orange juice perched on a tray, Rob headed back to his room.

Sipping the orange juice, Rob turned on his computer and waited for it to boot up. Yes, his personal Internet connection was very handy indeed!

Tom's e-mail was waiting for him.

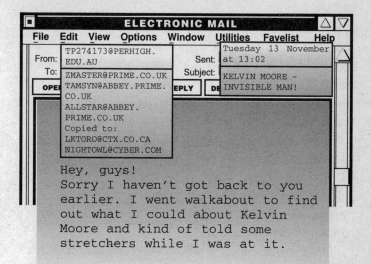

Rob smiled. "Stretcher" was Tom's term for stretching the truth. In other words, a lie!

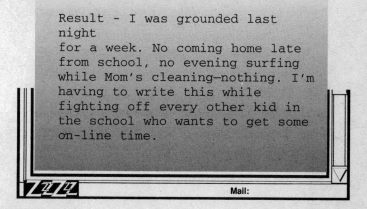

"Rob!"

Rob looked away from the screen as Mrs. Zanelli called him.

"Yes?"

Rob's mother popped her head around the door. "You haven't forgotten I'm taking you to school early today?" She looked at his pajamas and his half-eaten breakfast. "Yes, you have."

"Me?" said Rob, gulping down the remains of his cereal. "Nah! Give me five minutes . . . well, ten."

No time to read the rest of Tom's e-mail, decided Rob. Clicking on Print, he began getting his things together. By the time he'd done it, two sheets of paper had spilled out of his printer. Disconnecting from the Net, he stuffed them into his bag, then hurried out of his room and down the hall.

"Have you decided about this weekend?" Mrs. Zanelli asked once they were on their way.

Rob looked at her blankly, then remembered. "The Internet Show, you mean?"

"Do you want to come? You'd make a good demonstrator!"

Mr. and Mrs. Zanelli's company, Gamezone, had recently set up a World Wide Web site on the Internet. Through it, people tried out games and e-mailed comments about what they thought. The Zanellis were going to demonstrate this at the show.

Rob thought for a moment, then shook his head. Computer shows were always fun, but only when you had room to move. The trouble was that organizers of these events liked to pack in as many customers as they could. Rob wasn't sure he wanted to push his way through hordes of people again this year.

"I think I'll skip it," he said. "Tamsyn said I could spend the day at her place."

"She could come, too," said Mrs. Zanelli. "And Josh. There'd be plenty of room in the car for them."

"Going there, maybe." Rob laughed. "Not coming back. Josh would load us down with every free sample he could lay his hands on!"

Rob met Josh and Tamsyn just as they were pushing their way into English class.

"Any news from Tom about that company?" asked Josh at once.

Rob fished in the bag on his lap and pulled out the sheets of paper he'd printed earlier. "Yeah, I got this, but I didn't have time to read it."

At last they were all able to read what Tom had been leading up to:

```
Anyhow, what I found out was that Moore's
company is in B-I-G trouble! They owe taxes
and all sorts of things. When I got to the
ChecKMate offices on Queensbury Street, my dad
was there turning the place inside out along
with a couple of billion tax inspectors! They
were stripping the joint, taking away
everything they could lift. Seems like Moore's
gotten himself into money troubles trying to
come up with a super version of his champion
chess program, a thing called Black Knight.
To top it off, Moore's gone! According to Dad,
he's skipped the country—just dropped
everything and ran. They know he took a plane
```

to New York last Saturday, so he could be anywhere in the USA by now.

"Gone," said Josh. "Does that mean Alice and everyone else lost their money?"

Tamsyn nodded. "Sounds like it. If the company owes taxes, then they'll be going bust, won't they?"

"I don't know," said Rob. "It doesn't sound too good, though."

A general shuffling from the front of the class announced the arrival of Ms. Gillies, their English teacher.

"What if they find Moore?" said Josh. "Won't that settle things?"

"Not if he's taken the company's money with him, it won't!" said Tamsyn. "Anyhow, the company might not *have* any money. They might owe the tax people more than they're actually worth!"

Josh puffed out his cheeks. "If that's the case, I guess I'd have skipped the country as well!"

Skipped the country? Tamsyn looked again at Tom's e-mail: *He could be anywhere in the USA by now.*

"Rob," she whispered, "that guy at the airport. You know, Clark? What if we're right and he really did get that business card from Moore?"

"I don't see how else he could have gotten it." Rob shrugged. "Like we said, they probably met on the plane."

"But don't you see?" She looked at him. "If *that* was the way it happened, then it means that Moore isn't in New York anymore. He's here in England!"

From the front came Ms. Gillies's raised voice. "Rob Zanelli. Tamsyn Smith. Josh Allan. From the urgency of your discussion, I assume you're looking at the homework I gave yesterday about the descriptions of London life in *Oliver Twist*. Correct?"

Rob, Tamsyn, and Josh stopped talking and looked up. All three of them began pulling out their books.

But Tamsyn couldn't concentrate. "If Moore was going to come here, though," she hissed at Rob a couple of minutes later, "why wouldn't he come *straight* here? Why go to New York first?"

"Maybe he's got a business there as well," said Rob.

In front of them, Josh nodded. Leaning back, he whispered over his shoulder, "It's obvious. He went there first, sorted some things out, then flew here."

Tamsyn shook her head. There was something wrong, something that didn't quite fit. "Why?" she whispered. "Wouldn't he want to stay out of sight? Why turn up where he'd be expected? And besides, if he was going to make a run for it, wouldn't he have sorted things out before?"

"Maybe he didn't have time," said Rob.

"Maybe he didn't come to England at all," said Josh, just a little too loudly. "Maybe this Clark guy met him in New York."

Ms. Gillies had had enough. "Josh! To the front, please, where I can keep an eye on you." She pointed to an empty space near the door. "Rob, over there. And Tamsyn," she added with a glare, "if your book isn't open in two seconds flat, I will want to know the reason why!"

As Josh and Rob disappeared to opposite corners of the classroom, Tamsyn pulled her copy of *Oliver Twist* toward her. Good thing she'd read some at the airport, she thought.

Now, where was she? Riffling the pages, Tamsyn searched for her bookmark.

That was when she saw it: the credit card slip she and Rob had found in the jacket pocket that day.

Smoothing it out, she looked at the signature at the bottom.

K. M. Clark

That was what didn't seem right. If Kelvin Moore had met this K. M. Clark person, why would he have given him his business card at all? Surely the last thing a fugitive would want to do would be draw attention to himself.

Unless . . .

No, thought Tamsyn at once. The idea she'd just had was completely crazy. . . .

Abbey School
10:20 A.M.

"Tamsyn, that's the nuttiest idea you've ever had!"

Josh put one finger to the side of his head and turned it back and forth, corkscrew fashion.

Even Rob agreed. "It sounds pretty loony, Tamsyn."

"I know it *sounds* unbelievable," said Tamsyn, "but it does fit the facts."

Right after English they'd headed for the student lounge area, a large circular room with lots of wooden seats. It was a good place to meet and talk.

Josh went over to the soda machine nearby and fed in some coins. He came back with three cans. "Okay," he said to Tamsyn. "Let's hear it again. And take it slow."

"In that suit pocket were one of Moore's business cards and a credit card slip signed by somebody called Clark. Right?"

Josh and Rob nodded.

"So how did they both get there?" Tamsyn asked.

"Either Moore gave Clark his business card . . . ," said Rob.

". . . or Clark gave Moore his credit card slip," finished Josh.

Tamsyn put a finger in the air. "Question one, then: Why would Moore give Clark his business card? Answer: He wouldn't. It would have drawn attention to himself, and I don't think a man on the run would do that."

She put a second finger in the air. "So, take the other option. Why would Clark give Moore his credit card slip? Answer: He wouldn't. And he didn't! We saw that guy, Rob, before and after he put those new clothes on. He *must* have been the one who bought them."

"So his name was Clark," said Josh. "And he didn't necessarily meet Moore recently. He could have had that business card for ages."

"Maybe," said Tamsyn. She took it out. "But it doesn't look like it's all that old, does it?" The other two didn't argue. "Which brings me to my other explanation."

"Loopy-land," said Josh.

"Loopy or not, it fits. Moore and Clark are the same person!" She laid down the credit card slip and the copy of the sheet of letterhead that Tom had sent them over the Net. Although Rob and Josh looked no less convinced than they had when she'd first mentioned it, Tamsyn went on, "I know it sounds crazy, but look at those two signatures. Don't they seem similar to you?"

"No," said Josh. Rob shook his head, too.

"Not at all?" said Tamsyn, wanting them to see for themselves what she'd seen.

The two boys looked more closely. "The *K*'s and *M*'s look alike, I suppose," said Josh slowly.

"True," said Rob. "Both *K*'s look like a *V* with a leg sticking out, and the *M*'s are lopsided." He looked at Tamsyn. "Is that what you're getting at?"

Tamsyn nodded excitedly. They *had* seen the similarity.

"Think about it. What would you do if you were on the run?"

"Go underground," Rob said thoughtfully. "And what better way of doing it than by changing your identity?"

Tamsyn pulled out a sheet of paper and scribbled the roughest of world maps, showing just Australia, Britain, and the United States of America.

"He knows the police are going to be after him, so he travels to New York as Kelvin Moore." She drew a line from Perth to New York. "Then, when he gets there, he changes his identity somehow. . . ."

"How?" asked Josh. "You need passports and all sorts of papers to do that."

"I don't know. Maybe he had it all planned, but the tax people in Perth got on to him before he was ready."

Rob nodded. "Tom's dad did say it looked like Moore had dropped everything and run."

"So he gets to New York," Tamsyn went on, "becomes Clark, and hops on a plane to London—dumping his old clothes at the airport in the process! Come on, you two. It all fits."

Rob nodded thoughtfully. "And the police are left looking for him in the wrong country . . ."

"And under the wrong name," concluded Josh. "Cool!"

Rob finished his drink. Crushing his empty can and tossing it into the recycling bin, he said, "Of course, there's a pretty simple check we could do on this theory."

"What?" said Tamsyn.

"Follow me!"

Five minutes later they were in the computer lab, with Rob seated at a keyboard. In front of him the screen was displaying its home-page menu. Rob double-clicked on Net Navigator.

"He had an American Airways flight bag with him, right? And we saw him come straight from arrivals."

"At about half past ten."

"So allow him half an hour to pick up his luggage."

"He didn't *have* any luggage worth talking about. No suitcase, just those bags. That's another thing that was odd."

"Okay. We'll still give him half an hour to come through customs. If that's the case, then we should find an American Airways flight from New York landing at Heathrow just after ten o'clock in the morning."

"On the Internet?" said Josh, leaning forward for a better look. "How do you know?"

Rob smiled. "My dad's always hopping on planes. I've seen him do this dozens of times."

With quick movements of the mouse, Rob clicked through levels of the menu. Finally he was there.

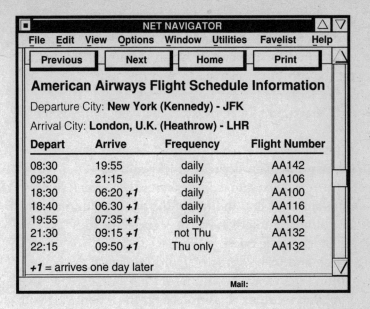

File   Edit   View   Options   Window   Utilities   Favelist   Help

| Previous | Next | Home | Print |

American Airways Flight Schedule Information

Departure City: **New York (Kennedy) - JFK**

Arrival City: **London, U.K. (Heathrow) - LHR**

Depart	Arrive	Frequency	Flight Number
08:30	19:55	daily	AA142
09:30	21:15	daily	AA106
18:30	06:20 *+1*	daily	AA100
18:40	06.30 *+1*	daily	AA116
19:55	07:35 *+1*	daily	AA104
21:30	09:15 *+1*	not Thu	AA132
22:15	09:50 *+1*	Thu only	AA132

+1 = arrives one day later

Mail:

Tamsyn looked eagerly at the screen. "Flight AA one-thirty-two," she said, pointing at the final line in the list. "That landed at nine-fifty. He could have been on that one."

Rob shook his head. "It's Thursday only," he said. "We were there on Sunday, remember?"

"And that flight gets in at nine-fifteen every other day of the week," said Josh. "If he was on that one he'd have already come and gone. You wouldn't have seen him."

"It was a nice idea, Tamsyn," said Rob. "Imaginative! But it doesn't seem to add up."

Tamsyn scanned the list again. They were right.

Apart from flight AA132, none of the other arrivals was even remotely close to the right time.

The bell for the end of lunch sounded. Rob turned off the computer as Josh opened the door.

"What have we got now?" he asked.

"Design and Technology," said Rob. "In this building."

Josh whistled. "That's lucky," he said, pointing out the window. The sky was murky and dark.

Even as she watched, Tamsyn saw a streak of lightning split the sky, and heard the boom of thunder follow almost immediately. She stopped dead.

"Storm!" she cried.

Rob and Josh stopped. "Duh, Tamsyn."

But Tamsyn was counting on her fingers. "Sunday, Rob! Bad weather conditions over the Atlantic. If your dad's flight was affected, then that American Airways flight from New York could have been, too. It wouldn't have arrived until *ten-fifteen*! Which means . . ."

"Moore . . ."

"Clark . . ."

"He *could* have been on it!"

She checked her watch. Just enough time. She turned back toward the computer lab.

"Where are you going?" called Josh.

"To e-mail Tom. We need a picture of that guy!"

CHAPTER 5

Perth, Australia
Wednesday, November 14, 8:15 A.M.

Tom was just finishing his breakfast as his dad came to the table.

"Any news about Kelvin Moore?" Tom asked at once. If there was, he could e-mail the others about it.

Mr. Peterson looked at him over a piece of toast. "Nothing yet. The New York police are checking out the usual places."

"Usual places?" queried Tom.

"Hotels, to see if he's stayed in any of them. Car rental companies, to see if he's rented a car and gone off somewhere else. Airports. It all takes time."

"You think you'll catch him? Drag him back?"

Mr. Peterson smiled. "I hope so. According to the tax people, he's cleared out his bank accounts. Probably stashed it all in an overseas account, maybe Switzerland."

"Tom, didn't you say you were catching the early bus?" said Mrs. Peterson.

Tom nodded and gulped down the last of his orange juice as he got to his feet. "I have to do some work," he said.

Mrs. Peterson's eyebrows rose. "I'm not sure I'd call sitting in front of a computer 'work,' " she said. "Anyway, get home on time. You're still grounded, remember. A minute late and you'll be grounded for another week."

Tom thought about asking his dad whether prisoners could have their sentences extended like that, but decided he didn't have time. Being grounded meant he couldn't get on the Net by staying after school or going with his mom in the evenings. That meant he had to beat the other kids to the school's one computer—and *that* meant catching the early bus!

He made it with seconds to spare. It was a regular bus, not a special school bus, and the first person Tom saw was Mr. Lillee, his teacher.

"Good morning, Tom," said Mr. Lillee. "Early bird, aren't you?"

"Hello, Mr. Lillee. Yeah, I've got a lot of work to do."

He headed on down the aisle toward an empty seat at the back of the bus. Ahead of him, Mr. Lillee had taken out his newspaper. Tom leaned forward, although he didn't have to. He could read the headline from where he was.

Disappearing Act

Businessman flees the country

Chess ace wanted for questioning by tax officials

Alongside it, there was a small photograph of a man. *Could that be Kelvin Moore?* wondered Tom.

He found out the answer ten minutes later, as the bus approached the stop opposite his school. Leaving his seat quickly, Tom tagged on to the end of the line of people standing in the aisle. He timed his move perfectly.

Just in front of him, Mr. Lillee still had his newspaper open. Tom was able to study the photograph. The man had a round face with a full mustache drooping down on both sides of his top lip. His hair was dark and shoulder length.

Beneath the picture was a caption. Tom bent forward to read it: "A recent picture of Kelvin Moore."

So that *was* him!

Tom leaped off the bus and dashed through the school gates, the thought of e-mailing the others with the latest developments making him run even faster. Clattering through the door and into the Resources

Room, Tom sat down in front of the school's only Internet computer and signed on.

At once he noticed the flashing Mail Waiting message in the bottom corner of the display. Tamsyn's note was waiting for him. Moments later he was reading, his mouth hanging open.

```
From: TAMSYN@ABBEY.PRIME.CO.UK
To: TP274173@PERHIGH.EDU.AU
Copied to: LKTORO@CTX.CO.CA
NIGHTOWL@CYBER.COM
Sent: Tuesday 13 November at 10:20
Subject: URGENT - KELVIN MOORE
```

Sent the day before! Again, Tom cursed the fact that he was grounded. Otherwise, he'd have seen this note last night.

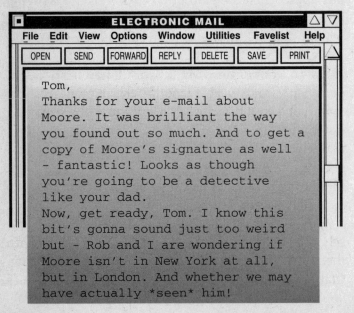

```
ELECTRONIC MAIL
File  Edit  View  Options  Window  Utilities  Favelist  Help
OPEN   SEND   FORWARD   REPLY   DELETE   SAVE   PRINT

Tom,
Thanks for your e-mail about
Moore. It was brilliant the way
you found out so much. And to get a
copy of Moore's signature as well
- fantastic! Looks as though
you're going to be a detective
like your dad.
Now, get ready, Tom. I know this
bit's gonna sound just too weird
but - Rob and I are wondering if
Moore isn't in New York at all,
but in London. And whether we may
have actually *seen* him!
```

Tamsyn's e-mail went on to tell Tom about what had happened, and about the business card and credit card slip.

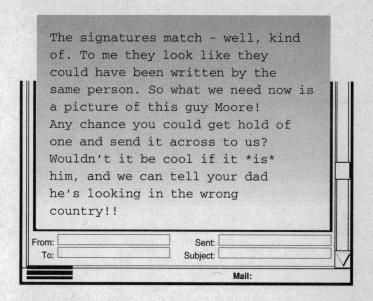

The signatures match - well, kind of. To me they look like they could have been written by the same person. So what we need now is a picture of this guy Moore! Any chance you could get hold of one and send it across to us? Wouldn't it be cool if it *is* him, and we can tell your dad he's looking in the wrong country!!

From:
To:
Sent:
Subject:
Mail:

A picture? thought Tom. *No problem!* He could dash out of school at lunchtime and buy a newspaper at the shop on the corner. He'd have enough time to scan the photo onto a diskette before school started again. Then he'd just have time to fire it over the Net at the end of school before catching his bus home.

First he should let Tamsyn and the others know he was on top of the situation. He clicked on the Reply icon.

Nothing happened. Instead of a screen panel opening up for him to type into, the display didn't alter.

He clicked on Reply again, then again.

"Come on, what are you doing?" he said aloud.

"Troubles?" said a voice. The technician responsible for the school's equipment, everything from chalkboard erasers to computers, had come to stand behind him.

"It's gone dead," said Tom.

The technician sighed. "The line's down again. Did that twice yesterday. I'll have to call the service provider to straighten it out. There's nothing I can do."

"What? How long will *that* take?" cried Tom.

The technician shrugged. "Couple of days, couple of weeks." He saw Tom's horrified look and gave him a serious answer. "Nah. Last time it took them a few hours. Probably be back up by the end of school. I'll schedule you for a half-hour at four, okay?"

"Four? What about half past three?"

The technician shook his head. "Already taken. It's four o'clock or tomorrow."

Tom wrestled with his problem. He had to get that picture across. But if he didn't get home on time, he was in trouble. Was there any way . . . ?

"You're on," he told the technician suddenly. "Four o'clock it is."

There *was* a way.

1:20 P.M.

Mr. Lillee's ritual before math class was well known. He would arrive in the classroom at quarter past one, dump his books and briefcase, then hurry off to make a quick cup of coffee. His newspaper would always be jutting out of the side pocket of his case.

On returning with his coffee, Mr. Lillee would then settle down to tackle the newspaper crossword for ten minutes before his students poured in for class at one-thirty.

Tom hung around in the corridor until he saw Mr. Lillee leave to make his coffee. Then he went into the classroom.

Slipping the newspaper from his teacher's brief-case, he took out the pair of scissors he'd borrowed from the secretary's office a little earlier. In next to no time he'd snipped the picture of Kelvin Moore from the front page. Then, turning to the back page, he cut out Mr. Lillee's half-completed crossword puzzle.

"That should do the trick!" Tom said to himself as he put the newspaper back where he'd found it.

By the time Mr. Lillee returned, Tom was standing in the corridor again. Part one of the plan was complete!

Ten minutes later he filed back into the room again, along with the rest of his class.

"Sit down quietly!" yelled Mr. Lillee.

"He doesn't look too happy," said the boy next to Tom.

Mr. Lillee got to his feet. Slowly he unfolded his newspaper. Holding it up so that the whole group could see the gaping hole Tom had cut in the front page, he gazed from side to side. "Who is responsible for this? And especially for this!" yelled the teacher, turning the newspaper around to show the gap in the back page where his crossword had been.

Around Tom a quiet tittering began as some of the class realized what Mr. Lillee was talking about. Tom tried to look as innocent as he could.

"Responsible for what, Mr. Lillee?"

"For this!" Now loud laughter echoed around the room as their teacher answered Tom's question by poking his hand through the hole in the back page.

"Quiet!" Mr. Lillee looked around slowly. "Is anybody going to own up?"

Tom stayed resolutely silent, but inside he was waiting impatiently for what he hoped would come next.

"All right. The entire class gets detention! Thirty minutes, after school today!" said Mr. Lillee.

Tom rejoiced. Mr. Lillee's standard punishment was well known to everybody—especially his mom. Part two of the plan was complete! He'd be out by four o'clock, ready for his Net time. And with the next bus home not until half past four, he'd be home as early as he could be.

It was turning into a good day after all.

Manor House, Portsmouth, England
Wednesday, November 14, 8:31 A.M.

Tom's message arrived just as Mrs. Zanelli called to say she was almost ready to leave. Quickly Rob clicked on Open.

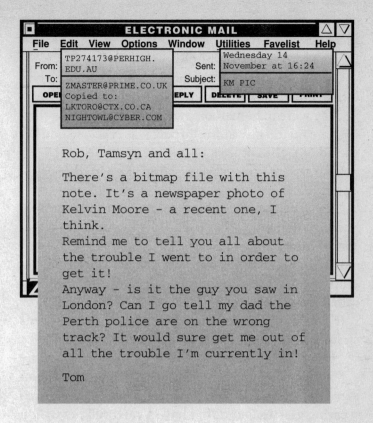

ELECTRONIC MAIL

File   Edit   View   Options   Window   Utilities   Favelist   Help

From: TP274173@PERHIGH.EDU.AU
To: ZMASTER@PRIME.CO.UK
Copied to:
LKTORO@CTX.CO.CA
NIGHTOWL@CYBER.COM

Sent: Wednesday 14 November at 16:24
Subject: KM PIC

OPE...   ...EPLY   DELETE   SAVE   PRINT

Rob, Tamsyn and all:

There's a bitmap file with this note. It's a newspaper photo of Kelvin Moore - a recent one, I think.
Remind me to tell you all about the trouble I went to in order to get it!
Anyway - is it the guy you saw in London? Can I go tell my dad the Perth police are on the wrong track? It would sure get me out of all the trouble I'm currently in!

Tom

"Are you ready, Rob?"

"Just a minute!"

Quickly Rob downloaded the bitmap file and printed it. As the sheet of paper oozed from the printer at the side of Rob's desk, he examined it. The picture had come out remarkably well. Tom had done a good, clean job of scanning it in.

There was only one thing wrong with it. . . .

"It isn't him, is it?" said Rob.

Tamsyn looked at the printed photograph of Kelvin Moore and shook her head. "No. Nothing like him."

They were in homeroom, waiting for the bell to ring.

"I mean, the guy at the airport was *behaving* oddly," she added. "But at least he looked pretty regular."

Rob raised an eyebrow. "And Kelvin the crook doesn't?"

"No way," said Tamsyn, poking the photograph. "Look at that mustache! Ugh! How can men grow that sort of thing?"

"My dad says it just happens," said a voice from behind them. "Unless you scrape it off with a thing called a razor."

It was Josh, his bulging backpack slung over his shoulder. He bent to look at the picture. "That him?"

"The one and only," said Rob.

"Nothing like the guy we saw at the airport," Tamsyn said. "Clark or whatever his name was. He was wearing glasses and didn't have a caterpillar crawling over his face."

"Tamsyn doesn't like mustaches," Rob said to Josh.

Josh looked down at the picture. "How about the earring?" he said.

"What?" said Tamsyn.

"Isn't that one?" said Josh, pointing at a small white spot on the man's earlobe. "No, maybe not."

"An earring! Rob, the man at the airport had a diamond stud, remember?" She bent low over the picture. "Is that one? Is it?"

Rob joined her. "Hard to say," he muttered. "The resolution's not good enough to tell for sure."

"And he's facing the camera," said Josh. He squinted hard. "But it could be. Yeah, I guess it could be."

"Coincidence, or what?" said Tamsyn.

Rob looked thoughtful. "I wonder what he'd look like without that mustache."

"And *with* a pair of glasses," Tamsyn added. She moved her head from side to side as she looked at the picture.

"Easy enough to find out," said Josh. "You've still got the bitmap file Tom sent, haven't you?"

Rob pulled a diskette from the bag attached to his wheelchair.

"So, why don't we put it through a graphics package? Edit out the mustache, give him some glasses . . . and see what happens!"

CHAPTER 6

Abbey School
12:40 P.M.

The picture of Kelvin Moore sat in the middle of the screen.

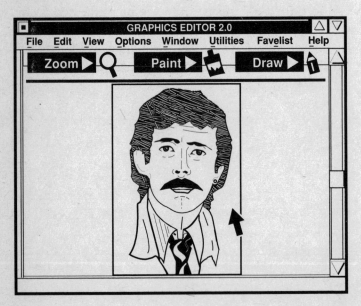

As Josh clicked the mouse button, a square box appeared on top of the picture. Moving the cursor to the center of the box, Josh pressed the left mouse button and held it down. A small icon of a hand shape appeared. Now, as Josh moved the mouse, the box moved, too. He positioned it just beneath Moore's nose.

"Size it," Tamsyn muttered. "It's not covering it all."

The box had eight small black blobs—one at each corner and one in the middle of each side. Putting the cursor on the blob in the middle of the right-hand side, Josh clicked and held again. This time he dragged the side so that the box became longer. With another couple of moves, the mustache was completely enclosed by the screen box.

"Now expand," said Rob.

Josh clicked on a magnifying glass icon. Immediately the area of the screen covered by the box was magnified, filling the screen with a mass of dots.

Tamsyn shook her head. "Amazing, isn't it? Take any picture, and it's just a load of black dots."

"Switch into edit mode," said Josh, clicking on another icon.

"And rub 'em out," said Rob.

Swiftly Josh took the mouse to dot after dot, clicking the mouse button as he went. Every click turned off a black dot. Ten minutes later, the job was finished.

"Can you give him a haircut?" said Rob. "The guy at the airport had much shorter hair."

"And don't forget his glasses," said Tamsyn, trying to control her excitement as she looked at the clean-shaven face on the screen. "A thick-rimmed pair. And make the lenses round, I think."

Josh removed dot after dot from the part of the display showing the man's hair until it looked much shorter.

Then bringing back the full display, he clicked on an icon showing a circle. Within moments he'd placed a couple of them over the eyes of the face on the screen, dragging the sides of each slightly to give them the shape of eyeglasses. Another short curved line across the bridge of the nose, a couple of straight lines back to the top of the ears, and it was done.

It was Rob who spoke first. "It is. It *is* him!"

Josh swung around in his seat. "You're sure?"

Tamsyn and Rob looked at each other, then once more at the face on the screen. "As sure as we can be," they agreed.

Josh whistled. "So. What do we do now?"

Nobody knew the answer to that question. "Well," Tamsyn said finally, "we could send *that*"—she tapped the screen picture—"to Tom. He could tell his dad what we think happened."

"Right," said Josh. "Then Mr. Peterson can give the police here in England a buzz and get them on the job. At least they'll be looking in the right country!"

As Tamsyn and Josh talked on, Rob leaned forward and began typing a note to Tom. Soon it was on its way, accompanied by the bitmap of Moore's edited face.

At the bottom there was a short addition, addressed to Lauren and Mitch.

```
Lauren, Mitch - thought you'd like to know
about this! Of course, we've got no idea if
he's still in England or not. Even if he is,
it doesn't help much. England might be pretty
small next to America or Canada, but it's
still big enough.
So, if you've got any ideas on how to go about
finding a Clark-in-a-haystack, let us know!
```

Toronto, Canada
8:15 A.M. (UK time 1:15 P.M.)

Lauren sat and stared at Rob's note, sent less than five minutes previously. Think of a way of tracking down a fugitive—it was a challenge, all right!

A general clattering from the kitchen area told Lauren that Alice was up and about. Soon she would be coming through the door with a breakfast tray piled high with waffles and maple syrup. Maybe that would help her think.

Lauren stood up and gazed out of the living-room window. It was going to be a fine day, crisp and cold. In downtown Toronto, the early-morning sun was already glinting off the glass of the massive 1,814-foot CN Tower.

It was strange to think that four hundred miles

southeast, Mitch might be reading the same e-mail and asking himself the same questions.

A sudden thought occurred to her. Turning back to the computer, Lauren returned to her home page and clicked on the menu item Utilities. When the drop-down menu appeared, she clicked on Talk. The screen was cleared, except for a dialog box in the center, which Lauren quickly filled in.

⚬ TALK TO WHICH USER ID? NIGHTOWL@CYBER.COM

If Mitch was logged on, he should answer quickly. . . .

New York, USA
8:19 A.M. (UK time 1:19 P.M.)

Mitch saw the request at once. He'd gotten in at quarter to eight, ready for a good forty-five minutes of surfing before his boss, Mr. Lewin, called him and gave him his list of jobs for the day.

Mitch worked as a just-about-everything at Cyber-Snax, a café on West 111th Street, close to the northern end of New York's Central Park. Cyber-Snax was a café with a difference, a high-tech place with ten Inter-net-linked computers. Surf While You Sip was Mr. Lewin's latest advertising slogan.

As far as Mitch was concerned, the Internet didn't need selling. The big attraction of working at Cyber-Snax was that in return for a bit of overtime, Mr. Lewin allowed Mitch to log on for free.

The request from Lauren came just after Mitch had
read the note from Rob.

```
TALK> REQUEST FROM LKTORO@CTX.CO.CA
          ANSWER Y OR N:
```

Mitch typed "Y." . . .

Toronto, Canada
8:20 A.M. (UK time 1:20 P.M.)

```
TALK> REQUEST ACCEPTED BY NIGHTOWL@CYBER.COM
```

Alice was just serving up breakfast as Mitch's re-
sponse came back. Sliding the tray onto a coffee table,
she pulled up a chair.

"Yak mode, huh?" she said.

"We call it direct Internet communication, Allie,"
said Lauren with a smile.

Alice nodded sagely. "Like I said. Yak mode."

Lauren started typing, clicking on the Send icon
every time she finished what she wanted to say. At
his end, she knew, Mitch would do the same. Their
conversation began, every line appearing on both
screens.

```
Hi, Mitch. You see Rob's e-mail? Any ideas?

  MITCH> Zilch, Lauren! Track down a
  fugitive? I've never been a fugitive.
```

Neither have I. I can't even imagine it. Hey,
maybe that's what we need to do - *imagine*
we're him. Say I came into New York from
Australia. What would I do first?

    MITCH> Easy one: crash. That's got to be
    a 24-hour flight, minimum! You'd be
    Zambo the Zombie at the end of that!

"Not counting the half-day time difference," said
Alice in Lauren's ear. "Midnight here and New York is
one in the afternoon in Perth."

"So what would he do?"

"I know what *I'd* do," said Alice. "Find a nice soft
bed!"

Lauren looked at her grandmother. Had Kelvin
Moore done the same?

Mitch, suppose he got in real late. What's the
easiest way to find a bed for the night in New
York?

    MITCH> Get a cab? No, strike that. I
    remember being out at JFK a while back.
    The place is just crawling with buses.
    Carey Airport Express buses, they're the
    ones. They cruise around some of the big
    Manhattan hotels.

Could you check them out?

    MITCH> What? You think I should just
    stroll into those places? What's with
    that idea?

"Good question," said Alice, wiping a dab of syrup from her chin. "What's your thinking?"

Lauren paused before answering. "I don't know, Allie. But if some of Moore's business was in chess programs then I'm wondering if he isn't a chess player himself."

"And?"

"And a good chess player," Lauren said, "thinks as many moves ahead as he can."

Alice nodded slowly. "Like moving from one house to another," she said. "Your grandfather and I moved so often, I had to check the number on the front door every time I went out in the morning."

Not for the first time in her life, Lauren wondered what Alice was leading up to. "I don't get you, Allie."

"When you move, you have to do a lot of planning," said Alice. She began counting off on her fingers. "Cancel utilities in one place, arrange for service in the other, pack things . . . and make sure the people you want to find you can find you."

"You mean . . . leave a forwarding address?" asked Lauren. "But why would he do that? He doesn't *want* anybody to find him."

"No?" said Alice. "I think he might. . . ."

As she listened, Lauren started typing again:

```
Mitch, when Moore landed in New York he was
using his own name. By the time he got to
England, he'd changed it to Clark. Allie and I
figure his plan was to start using his new
name while he was in New York, so that the
trail stopped there.
```

```
    MITCH> Sure. But why check out the
    hotels?


Because when you stay at one, you have to give
your address, don't you? So - maybe he gave
the address he was *going* to!


    MITCH> C'mon! Would that be dumb, or
    what?


Not if he was thinking a couple of moves
ahead. He couldn't give his Australia address,
and making up a false one could land him in
trouble if the hotel checked up on it. He
wouldn't have wanted that.


    MITCH> Could be. And hitting them with
    his real address gives him a back-door
    way of getting stuff sent on to him.
    Still a long shot, though.


I know. But what do you think?


    MITCH> I think I've got me a cruisin'
    job! Just call me the subway ranger,
    Lauren! I'll think of a way of checking
    them out.
```

"Do you think he'll find out anything, Allie?" said Lauren after Mitch had signed off to end their talk session.

Alice took a final bite of her cold waffle. "Doubt it. But like I always say: If you don't ask, you don't get."

Lauren glanced across at her breakfast, sitting cold

and unhappy on its plate. "That's true, Allie. So—any chance of a fresh waffle?"

Mitch Zanelli placed the bulging brown-paper-wrapped package between his feet and looked up at the towering glass skyscraper in front of him. On top of it stood a massive Times Plaza sign, which could be seen for blocks in either direction.

It was the eleventh, and last, hotel on Mitch's list.

He'd managed to get the afternoon off from Cyber-Snax, doing a swap with a dishwasher who didn't want to work the evening shift.

By just after 1 P.M. Mitch was cutting through Central Park on his way toward the subway station at the intersection of 86th Street and Lexington Avenue. From there it was a direct, spitting and crackling ride on the subway to New York's cavernous Grand Central Station.

It was there, Mitch had discovered, that the Carey Airport Express buses made their first stop. He'd waited until one drove up, then walked up to the driver's door.

"Hi!" said Mitch. "Which hotels do you go to from here?"

The man, his peaked cap pushed back on his head, glanced down at Mitch's stained Cyber-Snax sweatshirt, frayed jeans, and ancient sneakers. "Why are you asking?" he said with a laugh, a gold tooth flashing. "You looking for a room?"

Mitch grinned up at him. "My boss wants to know. He thinks he could get in there, y'know, put in some surfing systems."

"Huh?" The driver scratched his head as Mitch went on.

"But he's choosy, man. Only wants the ones with the most visitors. 'That's got to be the ones the Carey buses go to,' he says. So when I saw you, I thought I'd ask."

The driver nodded wisely. "He ain't wrong. Okay, from here I go to the New York Hilton. That's on Sixth Avenue. After that it's the Sheraton Manhattan on Seventh, then the Holiday Inn Crowne Plaza and the Marriott Marquis. They're both on Broadway. . . ."

Mitch was jotting down the names on a scrap of paper. He kept on scribbling as the driver reeled off another half-dozen names without pausing for breath before, finally, coming to the end of his list.

"Last stop is the Times Plaza, on Times Square, of course. Then it's back to the airport."

Revving his engine, the driver looked down at Mitch. "You got all that?"

Mitch barely had time to say thanks before the driver straightened his cap with one hand and pulled at the steering wheel with the other.

Eleven hotels. Mitch had set off for the first on his list . . . then the second . . . then the third . . .

Now, as he stood on the sidewalk outside the Times

Plaza, he wondered if he should even bother to go in and try his act.

It'll be the same as all the others, he thought. "K. M. Clark? Sorry. Nobody here by that name."

He looked across at the hotel entrance. Was it worth it? His feet ached, and so did his back from carrying his heavy package. But it was the last hotel. Promising himself a bagel from the place on the corner as soon as he came out, Mitch picked up the package.

Dipping into his pocket, he pulled out the remains of the wad of self-stick labels he'd brought with him. Peeling one off, he stuck it on top of the mound of labels that had grown since he started his tour.

He wrote on it:

MR. K. M. CLARK
c/o THE TIMES PLAZA

Then, as the crossing signal flashed Walk, he headed across Times Square.

The hotel's revolving door was the biggest he'd encountered all afternoon. Each compartment seemed big enough to accommodate an elephant, thought Mitch.

When he actually came through the door, he wasn't so surprised. The hotel lobby was large enough to hold a *herd* of elephants! From the ceiling hung crystal chandeliers. Plush seats were surrounded by potted palms, and the sheen of marble was everywhere.

Mitch was conscious of his tattered jeans and squeaking sneakers as he walked across the marble floor toward the reception desk in the corner of the lobby.

As he approached, the desk clerk looked up. "Yes?" she sniffed.

For the eleventh time that afternoon, Mitch said, "Got a package for Mr. Clark. Mr. K. M. Clark."

Without a word, the desk clerk turned to the terminal in front of her. Her quick fingers typed in a few characters. Almost at once she said, "The K. M. Clark who checked out Saturday morning?"

Mitch felt his heart begin to thump.

"That's the one," he said as innocently as he could. "And he checked out when, you said?"

"Saturday," repeated the desk clerk patiently. She turned away, as if that was that.

"Uh . . . hey . . . I've got this package for him."

"Looks like you'll have to send it, then."

"That's the bad news," said Mitch. "I don't have his address. He called with his order but didn't give another address, only this one."

The desk clerk ignored him.

Mitch leaned over the reception desk. "Do you have another address for him?"

"We do not disclose our guests' addresses," the clerk said at once.

So you have *got an address for him,* thought Mitch.

"C'mon, give me a break," he said. "One measly address. What's it to you? I mean, you'll be doing Mr. Clark a favor."

"No way," said the desk clerk.

Mitch thought hard. All he needed was a look at the

screen the desk clerk was using. The address must be on it.

But how? The reception desk was about two feet wide, with the clerk's screen perched on a lower shelf behind it. To get a look at it, Mitch had to get around to her side—or *over* to her side. . . .

Bending down, he lifted the heavy package he'd been lugging around all afternoon. "You gonna make me carry this back?" he complained. "Let me tell you, this is heavy. C'mon, try it for yourself."

He lifted the parcel up onto the marble top of the reception desk.

"I don't want—" began the clerk.

She didn't get a chance to finish. The moment he got the parcel onto the marble top, Mitch gave it a hefty push. Before the desk clerk could do a thing to stop it, the parcel had slid across to her side and over the edge.

As it fell to the floor with a sickening thud, Mitch reacted as though the end of the world had come.

"Oh, come on! You dropped my package! That's full of china! You dropped my package!"

"I didn't do anything!" screeched the clerk. She bent down to feel the brown wrapping.

It was the moment Mitch had been aiming for. Levering himself up onto the reception desk, he stretched right across it as if he was looking for a glimpse of his shattered package.

"Aw, I'm in deep trouble now," he moaned. But instead of looking down as the desk clerk concentrated on picking up the parcel, he turned his head around to look at what was displayed on her computer screen.

He had just enough time before the furious clerk stood up and slid the rattling parcel back to him. Mitch picked it up and shook it, a look of agony on his face.

"Have a nice day," said the woman.

Mitch turned away. He trudged slowly across the lobby and through the revolving door. Only then did he break into a sprint. If he got back to Cyber-Snax quickly, he'd have just enough time to get the address he'd seen across to the others.

Racing down into the subway, he launched the brown-paper-wrapped package into a nearby trash can. It split open. Out poured the collection of rocks he'd gathered on his journey through Central Park earlier that afternoon!

CHAPTER 7

Abbey School
Thursday, November 15, 8:45 A.M.

Mrs. Zanelli pulled her car into the school grounds. She unloaded Rob's wheelchair from the back, unfolded it, and brought it around to the passenger door. Rob slipped from one seat to the other with practiced ease.

"Have you checked with Tamsyn about Saturday?" Mrs. Zanelli asked him.

"Yes. It's fine. I can stay with her family until you get back. Josh will probably come by as well."

"Unless all three of you want to come to the show," said Mrs. Zanelli. "I know it gets crowded, but we'll find some room for you all in our booth. . . ."

Rob shook his head. "I'll pass, Mom, really. Put me down for next year!"

He wheeled his way across to the computer lab. From the thatch of dark hair jutting out above the corner machine, Rob saw at once that Josh was already at work.

"All right, Josh?"

He was answered by a groan. "Lauren King two,

Josh Allan zero. And games three, four, and five look like they're going the same way."

"Josh is getting mangled by the Toronto chess whiz," Rob said to Tamsyn as she came hurrying through the door. "Lauren's sent her latest crushing move."

"Did she say anything about Moore?" Tamsyn asked at once.

"Moore?" said Josh. "How about some sympathy for me first?"

"Poor you," said Tamsyn. "Now, what did Lauren say about Moore?"

"She sent a copy of an e-mail she'd fired off to Mitch. She and Alice think Moore would have needed to crash when he got to New York. Mitch was going to check out the big hotels, to see if he could find out anything."

Rob logged on quickly. Mitch's e-mail, written after the last customer had left Cyber-Snax, was there waiting for him:

```
                ELECTRONIC MAIL              △ ▽
   File  Edit  View  Options  Window  Utilities  Favelist  Help

                                      Wednesday 14
  From:  NIGHTOWL@CYBER.COM     Sent:  November at 23:54
  To:    ZMASTER@PRIME.CO.UK    Subject:
         Copied to:
  OPE    TP274173@PERHIGH.      EPLY  DELETE  SAVE  PRINT   FOUND HIM!!!!
         EDU.AU
         LKTORO@CTX.CO.CA

         Rob, my Zanelli-man, I got some
         news!

         Yesterday I trekked around to the
         big hotels. Nearly wore my
         sneakers through. But I found out
         that a K. M. Clark stayed at the
```

Times Plaza here in New York. He
checked out on Saturday the tenth
so he could have been the guy you
saw at the airport.

BECAUSE ... the address he gave
was a LONDON address!

I grabbed a look at the desk
clerk's screen. It was a real
quick look 'cause she was getting
ready to take my head off. All I
managed to spot were the words:
        Kensington and *London*
You know that area? Is it anywhere
near you guys? I didn't see a
house number, but I'm pretty sure
there was a street name. Oh, yeah,
and there was a phone number.
Something like 271-2789, with a
bunch of other numbers in front.

This any good?

Mitch (the trainee private eye)
Zanelli!

Mail:

"London," said Tamsyn. "Either of you two know
anything about London?"

"Only that it's awfully *big*," said Josh.

Rob shook his head slowly as he stared at the
screen. "I've heard of Kensington Palace. I'm sure I
have."

Tamsyn leaned across and flipped back to the

school's home page. "We must be able to use the Net somehow."

Josh got up from his seat and came over to join them. "Try Travel," he said.

"Why?"

"Because that's what Moore's done—traveled here. It might turn up something."

They clicked on Travel, just as they had when checking out the flight times. This time they noticed it also included information on accommodations.

"Try that," said Tamsyn. "If he came here in a hurry, then he'd have no place of his own to go to. He could have found a place to stay from the Net."

"And he stayed at a hotel in New York," said Rob. "Maybe he's at a hotel here too."

He clicked on Hotels, then, when he got a menu asking for an area of the country, selected London. A list of names appeared, in alphabetical order. It filled the screen, without even getting to the B's.

Rob hit page down. The list continued. He paged down again, and again . . .

"There's zillions," said Josh. "What do we have to do, check them all?"

"No, we can—" began Rob, only to be interrupted by the first class bell.

"Oh!" cried Tamsyn. "Why does school always have to get in the way?" She snatched up her book bag. "Let's meet here at lunchtime and do it then, okay?"

Josh looked uncertain. "How about the library? You could use their machine."

"What about you?"

"Me? I'll be looking for a chess book! I've got to get my next move for game four across to Lauren."

"No problem," said Rob. "We can do a search. It shouldn't take long. Then you can send your move."

"All right. I don't want to be late with it. She'll think I'm scared of getting beaten."

Tamsyn laughed as she opened the door. "But you are, aren't you?"

"Not anymore," said Josh. "I'm getting used to it."

Perth, Australia
7:05 P.M. (UK time 11:05 A.M.)

Tom leaped up as he heard the front door slam. Rushing down the stairs, he raced into the kitchen. Mr. Peterson was just pouring himself a cold drink.

"Any news about Kelvin Moore?" asked Tom at once.

To his son's delight, Mr. Peterson shook his head. "Nope. It's as if he vanished into thin air. We've got him on record all the way to New York. His flight went from Perth to Sydney, then on to Los Angeles in America. Then he got an internal flight to New York. After that, nothing."

Mr. Peterson took a swig of his drink. "The guys over there have been going through hotels, airline offices, credit card companies—the works," he added. "No sign of him."

Tom whipped out the sheet of printer paper he'd been holding behind his back.

"Dad, he hasn't. He's vanished to London!"

Mr. Peterson raised his eyebrows. He reached out and took Tom's paper.

Tom waited patiently. He'd found Mitch's note at the end of the afternoon, just before he'd left school, and printed it out at once. For the past three hours he'd been waiting for this moment, hardly able to concentrate on his homework.

As Mr. Peterson looked at Mitch's note, Tom explained about the man called Clark, whom Tamsyn and Rob had seen at Heathrow Airport.

Taking the letter from him, Tom showed his father the picture of Moore that Josh had edited to remove his mustache and add glasses. Then he showed him the printout of Clark's signature.

"Look at the *K* and *M* in 'K. M. Clark,'" he said. "Just like they are in 'Kelvin Moore'!"

Mr. Peterson looked at him. "How did you see Moore's signature?"

Tom gulped. The sheet of letterhead he'd picked up at the ChecKMate offices was still hidden in his crime drawer, and that was where it was going to stay for now. Almost pushing Mitch's note back into his dad's hands, he dodged the question altogether.

"Now this! Look—Kensington, London!"

Mr. Peterson picked up his drink as he read the note again.

"Well?" Tom said as Mr. Peterson put the sheet down. "What do you think?"

His father finished the rest of his drink. "I think," he said slowly, "it won't take more than a phone call to prove you've got it all wrong."

He flipped open his portable phone and punched in a number. Tom heard a couple of rings before it was answered.

"Hi, Carl. Can you do me a favor? See if you can find out who or what's at this number—271-2789. It's a London number. Kensington area. Oh, and Carl—don't say you're from the Perth police." Mr. Peterson couldn't quite stop himself from smiling as he added, "Just in case somebody named Kelvin Moore answers the phone."

Tom's dad snapped his phone shut. Leaving it on the kitchen table, he went upstairs to change. Tom didn't move. He sat and watched the phone, willing it to ring. Ten minutes went by. Twenty.

And then it rang.

Mr. Peterson was back in the kitchen at once. "Yes, Carl?" he said.

From the other end came a murmured explanation. Mr. Peterson nodded. "Fine. Thanks." He flipped the phone shut.

"What is it? Is he in London?"

"If he is," said Mr. Peterson, "then he's dead. That was the number of Kensington Crematorium!"

Abbey School
1:15 P.M.

"Kensington Crematorium?" Rob made a face. "You're sure?"

Tamsyn replaced the receiver on the pay phone outside the school office. "Of course I'm sure! It's not exactly something you can get wrong!"

During a dull moment in class, she'd thought of dialing the phone number Mitch had given them. Now she almost wished she hadn't.

"What next?" she said glumly.

"We go and do what we planned to do," said Rob, not appearing to be discouraged at all. "Mitch said he was in a hurry. He must have gotten the number wrong. Let's look at what's on the Net anyway."

Ten minutes later they'd logged on using the PC in the library. The search was quick. After tracing through the same route as they had that morning, and again reaching the large list of hotel names, Rob clicked on Utilities in the menu bar. A drop-down menu appeared. Rob clicked on Search.

Immediately a panel popped up:

SEARCH FOR?

Rob typed in "Kensington." At once the list of hotels changed. Instead of sprawling over many pages, the list was reduced to just under a screenful.

"Now what?" said Tamsyn.

"Check each of them," suggested Rob. "None of their phone numbers will match the one we've got. But we might find one that's close."

Rob began going through the list, clicking on each name in turn. Every time, a further screen came up giving details of the hotel. Sometimes it was just a simple page of text, with the hotel's address and telephone number together with the costs of staying there.

Other names brought up a much more complicated

screen, with a picture of the hotel and a page of text with underlined words.

"World Wide Web home page," said Rob as one came up.

Tamsyn nodded. She knew that behind the underlined words lay more information. All they had to do was click on the word to get it.

Rob was nearing the end of the list. Each of the hotels they'd looked at so far had *Kensington* in their file somewhere. Either their address was in Kensington, or *Kensington* was part of their name—often, both.

"Look!" Tamsyn said as Rob brought up the home page for the Kensington Continental Hotel.

"Close." Rob nodded. "The closest by far. 271-7289 instead of 271-2789."

"Guys! I've got it!" It was Josh, appearing from behind the library's reference shelves and sounding as if he'd found buried gold.

In his hand was a book: *Winning Chess*.

"The Lauren-beater, huh?" said Rob.

"Man, I hope so!"

"Castling . . . ," murmured Tamsyn. She was looking at the phone number on the screen. "Swapping pieces . . ."

"What about it?" said Rob.

"Mitch must have gotten the *digits* right, but in the wrong sequence. Maybe he accidentally swapped the seven and the two."

"And what he saw was part of the phone number for the Kensington Continental Hotel? Could be."

Together, they studied the hotel's home page. It gave rates for the different types of hotel rooms. "Expensive," whistled Tamsyn.

"Big," said Josh, looking over her shoulder. "Easy to stay out of sight in a place that size."

Rob had a nagging feeling at the back of his mind. "That name's familiar," he said.

Why? he wondered. He scanned the page. At the bottom, there was a line reading Conference Center: Forthcoming <u>Events.</u> Idly Rob clicked on the underlined word.

"Isn't that the show your mom was asking us to go to?" said Tamsyn.

"Yes!" exclaimed Rob. "*That's* why I'd heard of it before. The Kensington Continental is where it's being held."

"And you think Moore could be there?" said Josh. "Come on! He's supposed to be keeping a low profile, isn't he?"

"If he's under a false name, he *is* keeping a low profile," said Tamsyn. A thought occurred to her. "What goes on at one of those exhibitions, Rob?"

"Buying and selling," said Rob. "Companies set up booths and show off their stuff, take orders, that kind of thing."

"Take orders?"

"Sure. A lot of money changes hands."

Tamsyn looked at the screen again. Down at the bottom there was an underlined phrase: <u>Companies taking part.</u> Taking the mouse from Rob, she clicked on it. A list came up. She scrolled down until she reached the section beginning with the letter *C*.

Silently, she pointed at a name on the screen. Rob and Josh both looked at her.

"You know, Tamsyn, I've changed my mind," Rob finally said. "I'd like to go to that show after all. How about you?"

"Me too," said Tamsyn. "Josh?"

"Count me in," said Josh at once. "That is *too* big a coincidence."

They all looked again at the screen—at the name that seemed to leap out at them:

```
CheckMate Inc.
```

Perth, Australia
Friday, November 16, 12:45 P.M.

Tom didn't know what to do. He read Tamsyn's note again.

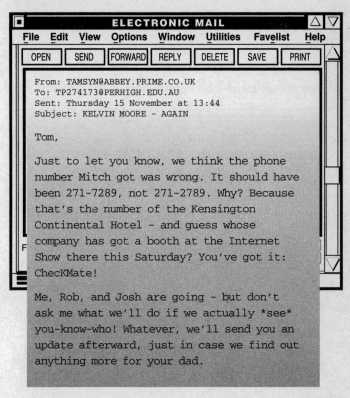

```
ELECTRONIC MAIL

File  Edit  View  Options  Window  Utilities  Favelist  Help

OPEN  SEND  FORWARD  REPLY  DELETE  SAVE  PRINT

From: TAMSYN@ABBEY.PRIME.CO.UK
To: TP274173@PERHIGH.EDU.AU
Sent: Thursday 15 November at 13:44
Subject: KELVIN MOORE - AGAIN

Tom,

Just to let you know, we think the phone
number Mitch got was wrong. It should have
been 271-7289, not 271-2789. Why? Because
that's the number of the Kensington
Continental Hotel - and guess whose
company has got a booth at the Internet
Show there this Saturday? You've got it:
CheckMate!

Me, Rob, and Josh are going - but don't
ask me what we'll do if we actually *see*
you-know-who! Whatever, we'll send you an
update afterward, just in case we find out
anything more for your dad.
```

Tom printed out the note. He didn't know whether to show it to his dad. Just thinking about the Kensington Crematorium disaster made him blush.

He tore the page from the printer and stuffed it in his pocket. *I'll show it to him,* he thought. *Maybe . . .*

CHAPTER 8

Kensington Continental Hotel
Saturday, November 17, 10:30 A.M.

The signs to the exhibition had started two miles away, small yellow signs attached to streetlights at regular intervals. Now, as Mrs. Zanelli swung her car around a final turn, they saw another: The Internet Show— Parking.

Mrs. Zanelli ignored it. Instead, she drove up to the hotel's main entrance and stopped there. A uniformed doorman began to wag a finger, but when he saw Rob's wheelchair in the back, he hurried forward to help.

"You three go on in," said Mrs. Zanelli to Rob, Josh, and Tamsyn. "I'll go and park the car. You've got your tickets?"

Tamsyn held them in the air.

"Fine," said Mrs. Zanelli. "I'll meet you in the refreshments area in a couple of hours."

As she hopped back into the car and headed for the underground parking garage, the three friends went into the large hotel lobby with its smooth polished floor. Gentle music was playing from somewhere above.

"Conference center's that way," said the doorman, pointing off down a long corridor.

"Thank you," said Rob. "Um . . . my mother has a friend staying here. Is there any way we can find out his room number?"

The doorman shook his head. "Sorry, we don't give out room numbers. Hotel policy." He stepped toward a small information desk at the side. "I can call him on his room telephone, though. Get him to come down and meet you. What's his name?"

"Clark," said Rob at once. "Mr. K. M. Clark."

"What are you doing?" whispered Tamsyn as, with two slow fingers, the doorman began typing on a small terminal. "What are you going to say if he does come down?"

"Tell him he's the wrong Mr. Clark, of course!" said Rob.

But instead of reaching for the phone on the information desk, the doorman was looking at the screen and shaking his head.

"Sorry. He checked out this morning."

"Already?" said Josh. "So he *was* here?"

"Oh yes." The doorman nodded. He looked again at the screen. "Since Sunday. Did he know you were coming?"

"No," said Rob. "We were going to surprise him. Ah, well . . ."

Turning away, the three friends began to head across

the lobby toward the corridor leading to the conference center.

"Well, at least we got something right," said Tamsyn. "Clark *was* here."

Josh shrugged. "So that's it, isn't it? He's come and gone."

Suddenly Rob stopped. "Maybe not," he said. "Look over there. Let's check it out."

Next to a square pillar was a pile of suitcases. A large net had been placed over the top of them.

"Why?" said Josh.

"Hotel guests have to check out by this time in the morning or they get charged for another day," said Rob. "Dad always has a fit about that, especially if he's booked on an afternoon flight. He says there's nothing else he can do but hang around the hotel until the bus comes to take him to the airport."

Tamsyn glanced at the pile of luggage. "And you think Clark's suitcase might be there?"

"With his name on it?" said Josh. "Come on. He'd want to keep that quiet, wouldn't he?"

"Josh," said Tamsyn, "Clark is his new identity. Why should he keep that quiet? It's Moore they're looking for, not Clark."

"It's worth a look, isn't it?" said Rob.

On the other side of the pillar, a waiter was serving coffee to a woman wearing a red suit. Unnoticed by the three friends, the woman looked up as they began to circle the suitcase pile.

"What are the stickers for?" asked Tamsyn. Every

suitcase bore a colored sticker, cases with the same color being grouped together.

"For the bellhop's benefit," said Rob. "Different color, different bus to the airport."

"Clark, Clark," muttered Tamsyn as she walked sideways, reading the tags hanging from each case. "Hey! Come here!"

Rob and Josh quickly joined her. There, hanging from the handle of an elegant new brown leather suitcase with a green sticker, was a tag bearing the name K. M. Clark . . . and an address.

"Switzerland!" said Rob. "He's going to Switzerland! Crooks stash their money in Swiss bank accounts, don't they?"

"If he *is* a crook," said Josh. He leaned against the pillar. "I mean, we still don't know for sure if this Clark guy really is Kelvin Moore."

"I know we don't," said Tamsyn. "But it fits together. And if we can spot him here somewhere and prove somehow that Clark isn't his real name . . ."

"How?" said Josh.

"I don't know how!" Tamsyn said hotly.

Rob held up a hand. "Take it easy! We've got to find him first. He must be around somewhere if his suitcase is still here. And my money's on the Internet Show."

"So what are we waiting for?" said Tamsyn, ready to set off.

Josh looked doubtful. "Shouldn't somebody stay here—in case he comes back?"

Tamsyn looked at Rob. "I vote we stick together."

Rob thought for a moment. "Me too," he said finally. "If this show's as crowded as the others I've been to, it'll take all three of us to spot him."

Josh elbowed himself away from the pillar. "Okay, let's go. Kelvin Moore, we're on your trail!"

Behind the pillar, the woman in the red suit watched for a moment as the three kids set off across the hotel lobby and toward the corridor leading to the conference center.

Then, leaving her coffee, she stood up and followed them.

The corridor led into what amounted to another, smaller lobby. This one was packed. On the far side, a crowd of people was milling around a counter with a Registration sign hanging above it. Beyond that point was a huge, brightly lit hall.

"This is chaos," said Josh, indicating the crowd at the registration desk. "Forget spotting anybody. We won't even get *in*!"

Rob shook his head. "We've got company tickets from Gamezone. We can go straight through."

Tamsyn handed their tickets to a man at the entrance. In return she received three glossy brochures. They were plans of the hall. Tamsyn gave one each to Rob and Josh.

"Booth M-twenty-seven," groaned Rob, looking at his plan. "It would be."

"What's wrong?" Tamsyn asked.

"The ChecKMate booth's on the mezzanine floor," Rob replied.

"On the what?" said Josh.

Rob pointed at the plan. It showed that as well as the large central hall, a lot of booths were on the floor above it. "The mezzanine floor. It's the one that goes all the way around, like a balcony."

"So what's the problem?"

Rob tapped the sides of his wheelchair. "No wings, man. We'll have to find the elevator."

"There," said Tamsyn, spotting a sign. They followed it to an alcove and found the elevator. Tamsyn pressed the button, and the doors swished open at once.

Josh pushed Rob's chair inside, and Tamsyn followed. She pressed the button marked *M*. The doors began to close—then sprang open as an arm was thrust through.

"Sorry," said a woman in a red suit. "Top floor for me."

The elevator rose slowly, then stopped again. Rob, Tamsyn, and Josh got out. Above them, a panel of lights showed the elevator going up to the top floor. By the time the three friends had moved off, it was on its way down again.

Seconds later, the woman in the red suit stepped out of the elevator on the mezzanine floor and looked around.

"The ChecKMate booth's this way," said Tamsyn, gesturing to the left.

Josh held back. "I don't see any point in going to see it," he said.

"Why not?" asked Rob.

"If he *is* here," said Josh, "he won't be turning up at that booth, will he? I mean, it'd be kind of dumb, wouldn't it? He might as well stand on a chair and shout, 'Come and get me!' "

"Josh is right, Tamsyn," said Rob. "He wouldn't dare show his face. I bet his own workers would like to get their hands on him, as well as the police. He's got their money too, remember."

Tamsyn stopped, almost bumping into a woman in a red suit. "Sorry," she said. The woman simply smiled, then walked over to stand at the mezzanine rail, where she stood looking down at the milling crowds in the main hall. Tamsyn turned back to answer Rob's point.

"How do we know Moore didn't have an accomplice?" she said. "That could be why he's here—to meet him."

"Or *her*," said Josh. "There are such things as female crooks, you know!"

"Okay, so he could be here to meet an accomplice," said Rob. "But do you really think he's going to take the chance of turning up at that booth?"

Tamsyn shook her head. She couldn't think of any reason why Moore would do such a thing. "No," she said, "but it's still worth having a look around."

"What for?"

"To find out if anyone is talking about him."

Rob nodded. "That makes sense. And *that* might be why he'd take the chance to be here—to see if he could pick up any news of the hunt for him."

They moved on, following the railing of the mezzanine. Down below in the main hall the crowds were building up, thronging the many booths.

On the mezzanine level, the booths were spaced evenly. Each of them was like a small, open-fronted shop with either displays or equipment or both. All had one or more people working in them, giving out advertising brochures or free gifts.

"I'm doing well here," said Josh, taking the third pen he'd been offered.

Rob was looking down at the plan on his lap. "M-twenty-three... M-twenty-four. It should be just up here," he said.

Ahead of him Tamsyn slowed, walked a bit farther ... then stopped.

Stand M-twenty-seven was almost completely bare. The only thing on display was a sign, hastily written on a white board:

CheckMate
NOT EXHIBITING

"There goes that idea," said Rob.

"I did say he'd be crazy to come here," said Josh.

Tamsyn looked at him. "But we saw his suitcase in the lobby, Josh. He *has* come here."

"So he *is* crazy!" said Josh.

"No, he's not, Josh," said Rob. He was looking

thoughtfully at the sign. "I think he's playing this whole business like a game of chess."

"What do you mean?" Tamsyn asked.

"By keeping his opponent guessing. This show would be an obvious place for the police to look for him. So what does he do to send them away?" Rob pointed at the sign. "Makes them think he's not here at all."

Josh looked unconvinced. "Yeah, but . . . if the ChecKMate stand's not in business, why *else* would Moore come here? What would be the point?"

He was interrupted by an announcement over the loudspeaker system.

"Your attention, please. The Internet Chess Challenge, with grand master Georgi Borzov, will be starting in one hour. Georgi will be competing simultaneously over the Internet against five chess-playing computer programs . . ."

"I mean—" Josh went on, only to be stopped by Tamsyn's frantic "Shhh!" as the announcer began to reel off the names of the different programs Georgi Borzov would be playing against.

". . . SuperChess from MicroLevel Software, Best Move from Paragon Systems, Black Knight from ChecKMate . . ."

"Black Knight!" cried Tamsyn. "*That's* why Moore would want to be here! To see Borzov play against the chess program he designed!"

Even as she said it, Tamsyn rushed to look over the mezzanine rail. After stopping to listen to the announcement, people had already begun to move toward a booth in the center of the main hall.

"That must be the one." Rob pointed as he and Josh moved to Tamsyn's side.

From above, they could see that the booth was open on all four sides. At one end, a bank of monitors had been set up. Around the other three sides were tables joined together in a U shape. On these tables Josh could see at least ten black-and-white boards.

Even as they watched, more people were heading toward the booth.

"It's him! There he is!"

"Where?" Rob and Josh were both looking down, their heads moving from side to side.

Tamsyn pointed toward the center booth. "There! The guy with the jacket."

"You're right," said Rob. "It *is* him."

With his jacket slung casually over his shoulder, the man they'd seen at the airport was moving toward the Internet Chess Challenge booth.

"So what are we going to do?" said Josh.

The three friends looked at one another. Now that it came down to it, what *were* they going to do? Josh took the lead.

"Think chess!" he said. "Surround him! There's three of us."

Rob nodded. "Right, Josh! But I can't get down there. I'll go back to the hotel lobby and park myself near his suitcase. That way if he gives you two the slip, I'll try to delay him."

"Good idea," said Tamsyn. As Rob headed for the

elevator she looked over the rail again. The man was getting closer to the Chess Challenge booth. "Josh, somehow we've got to get that guy to admit he's Kelvin Moore."

"And how are we going to do that?"

Tamsyn shook her head. "I don't know. But the first thing is to get near him."

"Okay," said Josh. "I'll go down."

"And I'll stay here and keep him in sight," said Tamsyn. "If you can't spot him when you get down there, look up at me. I'll guide you to him. When I see you're with him, I'll come down and join you."

As Josh raced off, Tamsyn fixed her gaze firmly on the man down below in the main hall.

She was concentrating so hard that she didn't even notice a woman in a red suit standing no more than six feet away from her at the mezzanine rail. The woman was gazing down into the main hall as well.

CHAPTER 9

Josh pounded down the stairs and into the bustle of people. Elbowing his way through the crowds, he headed as quickly as he could in the rough direction of the Chess Challenge.

Finding one aisle almost completely blocked, he looked up. For a moment he wondered if Tamsyn could see him. Then Tamsyn made a pointing motion with her hand, indicating that he should turn right. Ducking down into a much clearer aisle, he found himself at the farthest corner of the booth, virtually at the front.

He looked up again. Tamsyn had her thumb in the air. Josh turned slightly—and saw he was standing almost next to Clark! The diamond stud in his ear glinted in the bright lights.

At that moment the loudspeaker boomed again. "Ladies and gentlemen, Georgi Borzov!"

On the platform, in front of the bank of monitors, an announcer with a microphone in his hand was introducing a square, thick-set man. Clark joined in as the crowd gathered around the booth applauded.

The announcer went on. "And now, a special announcement. Before Georgi plays his Internet Chess Challenge, he has kindly offered to play ten other matches live, here at the Internet Show!" The announcer waved an arm at the chess boards arranged in a U.

An appreciative murmur went through the crowd. Georgi Borzov beamed. A movement at his shoulder caught Josh's eye. Clark was edging forward.

"Ten challengers are needed," the announcer said. "If you want to test your chess skills against Georgi Borzov, take a seat!"

As the announcement was made, Josh saw Clark hesitate for a moment. Then, with one firm step forward, Clark sat down at the nearest chess board.

Josh's action was instinctive. Without giving it a thought, he sat down at the next board. Only as the crowd surged forward, surrounding him, did it sink in. He, Josh Allan, who couldn't even give Lauren a decent game, was about to take on a chess grandmaster!

He looked up at Tamsyn but saw only a woman in a red suit. Then he saw that Tamsyn had left her spot at the mezzanine rail and was already hurrying toward the stairs.

"Make your opening moves!"

The sound of the announcer's voice jerked Josh into action. He looked down at his board.

Up on the mezzanine floor, he missed seeing the woman turn away and hurry after Tamsyn.

Tamsyn started to push through the crowds in the main hall, then stopped to look back. Yes, she was right! Behind her, the woman in the red suit had just reached the bottom of the stairs and was heading her way.

Why? It was only as she'd noticed the same woman leave the mezzanine rail and follow her that Tamsyn had realized that she seemed to have been near them ever since they left the hotel lobby. In the elevator, along the mezzanine walkway, by the rail—and now in the main hall itself.

Was it her imagination, or was she being followed? *This will prove it one way or the other*, thought Tamsyn. Ducking into the crowd around the Chess Challenge booth, she shouldered her way forward. A few "excuse mes" and black looks later, she reached Josh.

She glanced behind her. The woman in the red suit was pushing through the audience toward them.

"I think we've got problems," she whispered into Josh's ear.

"You can say that again!" Josh hissed back, a look of panic in his eyes. "I've made only five moves and I've lost my queen already!"

Inside the U, Georgi Borzov was moving quickly

from one chess board to the next. Thinking briefly, he'd make his move, then go to the next table.

Josh slid a pawn forward. When Borzov reached Josh's board, he stopped for an instant, moved a knight, then went on. Next to him, Clark caused him to stop for longer. Borzov stood thinking.

Tamsyn glanced behind her again. "I think we're being followed."

Josh looked at her. "What? Who by?"

"I don't know who she is. But I think we should get out of here fast."

Tamsyn stole a glance at the man beside Josh. Was he Kelvin Moore? If they could only get him to reveal himself somehow, that would be enough. They could run for it then. *But how?*

Borzov was on his way back again. Tamsyn felt an arm brush hers. She glanced to her side. It was the woman in the red suit! Whatever they were going to do, it had to be now!

She leaned forward as Georgi Borzov arrived at Josh's board. Taking one of Josh's rooks in a flash, the chess grandmaster grunted, "Checkmate."

Next to Josh, the man they knew as Clark glanced his way. "Bad luck, kid."

It was Tamsyn's chance. "ChecKMate," she said in a clear voice. "That's the name of your company, isn't it, Mr. Moore?"

"Yeah, that's right."

As the words slipped out before he could stop himself, a look of confusion crossed Kelvin Moore's face.

The look turned to panic as, beside Tamsyn, there was a sudden movement. It was the woman in the red suit. Stepping forward, she held out a badge for Moore to see.

"Detective Sergeant Pat Thompson. Kelvin Moore, I arrest you—"

She got no further. With a sudden thrust of his arm, Moore pushed her aside and slammed his seat backward. Shocked by the suddenness of it all, the crowd parted. Before anybody could stop him, Moore was racing out of the main hall and down the corridor leading to the lobby of the Kensington Continental Hotel.

From his position by the pillar, Rob saw the van draw up outside the glass doors of the hotel.

The doorman saw it, too. Crossing the smooth floor of the lobby, he began to peel off the net covering the mound of suitcases. Quickly the doorman began loading those with blue stickers onto a flat cart, ready to take them out to the van.

Moore's case has a green sticker, Rob noticed as the doorman moved it, not onto the cart, but to one side. *He must be booked on a later flight.*

It was at that instant that Moore burst into the hotel lobby, racing toward the suitcase mound and shouting, "Out of my way!"

Automatically the doorman stepped back. Moore pushed past him, pulling suitcases aside as he tried to find his own.

"Hey, hey!" cried the doorman.

He must know we're on to him! realized Rob. Something must have happened back in the conference center to make him panic. As he saw Tamsyn and Josh come racing in from the corridor, Rob knew that he was right.

Moore was still frantically looking for his suitcase, not realizing it had been moved to the side. Suddenly he saw it.

Rob moved quickly. Jerking his wheels forward, he caught Moore's suitcase between his footrests and began sliding it across the lobby floor.

Tamsyn and Josh saw Moore start to chase Rob.

"Stop!" screamed a woman. Detective Sergeant Thompson, the woman in the red suit, was racing toward the hotel's revolving door.

Seeing her, Moore abandoned his chase after Rob. Spinning around, he too began to run toward the door.

"He's getting away!" cried Tamsyn.

"Then grab this! Quick!" It was Josh—and in his hand was one corner of the net that had been covering the suitcases. Bending down, Tamsyn picked up the other corner.

Moore was almost on top of them, heading for the door.

"Now!" yelled Josh.

With as much strength as they could muster, Tamsyn and Josh launched the net into the air and over Moore's head.

Desperately the wanted man tried to struggle free, only to entangle himself even more.

As the net wound itself around his ankles, Kelvin Moore lost his balance and fell to the floor with a loud cry. Within seconds, Sergeant Thompson had him pinned to the ground.

It was all over.

Kensington Continental Hotel, London
13:35 P.M.

"Well done," said Sergeant Thompson, looking at Rob, Tamsyn, and Josh in turn. "All of you."

The three friends grinned at one another and at Mrs. Zanelli, who'd seen Tamsyn and Josh rushing to the hotel lobby.

"As you saw from the tag on his suitcase, Rob," said the detective, "he was on his way to Switzerland. Another couple of hours and we'd have missed him."

Rob turned to Josh and Tamsyn. "I feel like I've turned up in the middle of a movie. So tell me—what happened after I left?"

"You can all tell me," said Mrs. Zanelli. "I've missed the *whole movie!*"

They quickly explained about all that had happened since they'd first seen Moore at the airport.

"So that was why you suddenly changed your minds about coming to the Internet Show," said Mrs. Zanelli.

Rob looked sheepish. "We didn't want to say anything in case we'd gotten it all wrong."

"When we spotted Moore in the crowd, we just

wanted to prove for sure that he was who we thought."

"So I ended up facing Borzov the Brilliant," laughed Josh.

Tamsyn looked at the woman in red. "And then I spotted you, Sergeant Thompson, and thought you were following us."

"I was."

"But why?"

"A call came in to the department late yesterday from the Perth police—a detective there named Peterson."

"Tom's dad!" cried Tamsyn. "Tom must have told him about the telephone number!"

Sergeant Thompson went on. "Detective Peterson asked if we could spare somebody to come here, just in case there was anything to it. I got the job. I found out from the desk clerk that Clark had gone, and was just thinking about what to do next when I overheard you three talking about Moore. So, Tamsyn, following you is exactly what I *was* doing!"

"And when we got Moore to let slip who he really was . . . ," said Tamsyn.

"I stepped in," finished Sergeant Thompson with a smile. "Case complete!"

"What will happen to Moore now?" asked Rob.

"Sometime soon he'll be getting on another plane. Not the one he expected to catch today, though. A plane back to Australia."

Perth, Australia
Monday, November 19, 8:46 P.M.

Tom Peterson heard the welcome sound of his mother's cleaning bucket out in the school corridor.

No more lining up to get some on-line time on the Net. He wasn't grounded anymore. He was back in favor, coming into school to surf as much as he wanted while his mother worked.

He logged onto the e-mail system and began his note.

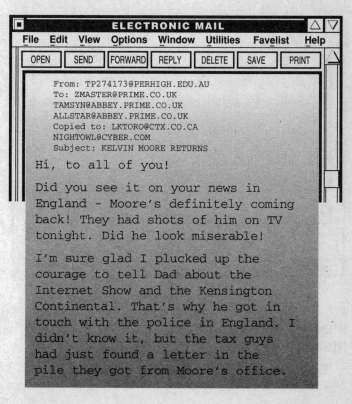

```
ELECTRONIC MAIL
File  Edit  View  Options  Window  Utilities  Favelist  Help

OPEN  SEND  FORWARD  REPLY  DELETE  SAVE  PRINT

    From: TP274173@PERHIGH.EDU.AU
    To: ZMASTER@PRIME.CO.UK
    TAMSYN@ABBEY.PRIME.CO.UK
    ALLSTAR@ABBEY.PRIME.CO.UK
    Copied to: LKTORO@CTX.CO.CA
    NIGHTOWL@CYBER.COM
    Subject: KELVIN MOORE RETURNS

Hi, to all of you!

Did you see it on your news in
England - Moore's definitely coming
back! They had shots of him on TV
tonight. Did he look miserable!

I'm sure glad I plucked up the
courage to tell Dad about the
Internet Show and the Kensington
Continental. That's why he got in
touch with the police in England. I
didn't know it, but the tax guys
had just found a letter in the
pile they got from Moore's office.
```

It was from the Internet Show
organizers, telling Moore that
Black Knight was going to be one
of the programs Georgi what's-his-
name played against.
Dad can't believe how it all
worked out. Neither can I! I've
been let off for swiping that
sheet with Moore's signature on,
my grounding's been lifted - and
Dad says there might even be some
loot coming along in the way of a
reward!

If it turns up I'll be sending it
to you, Allie. There's no way
you'll get your money back from
Moore, but at least you'll be
square. Hang on to it, though. It
said on the news that there could
be a buyer for Moore's set-up.
Lauren, you could get your chess
tutor yet!

Tom 'Sherlock' Peterson

| From: | | Sent: | |
| To: | | Subject: | |

Mail:

Abbey School
Monday, November 19, 1:40 P.M.

"Hey, Josh!" called Rob. He and Tamsyn had just seen
Tom's e-mail.

Josh looked up from the notepad he was writing in, his chess set at his side.

"A message from Tom has just come in. There's good news and bad news. Which do you want first?"

"The good news," said Josh.

"Moore's going back to Australia."

"Great. So what's the bad news?"

"Lauren might still get her chess CD-ROM."

Josh grinned. "No problem."

"How come?" said Tamsyn.

"Guys, remember you're talking to a man who's been beaten in six moves by the one and only Georgi Borzov."

"And that's good?" inquired Rob.

Josh tapped the notepad at his side. "It is if you've written down how he did it! Game six against Lauren starts today!"

Coming in December:
Internet Detectives #3

SPEED SURF

Gis Igne's ypm Gxliqy.
H$'s sssli3g a zqcht
c=@l2d #wMqo zmi Ojr.

The message on the computer screen is
nonsense. But it's the last message Josh
Allan, Rob Zanelli, and Tamsyn Smith receive over the Internet from a yachtsman
alone at sea—and they're sure it contains
a clue to the identity of an international
art thief. Now they must decipher the
scrambled message and, with time running
out, set a trap for a dangerous enemy.

SWEEPSTAKES OFFICIAL RULES

I. ELIGIBILITY

No purchase necessary. Enter by completing and returning the Official Entry Form, or hand print your name, address, and birthdate on a 3"x 5" card, and mail it to Bantam Doubleday Dell, Attn: Internet Detectives Computer Sweepstakes, 1540 Broadway, 20th Floor, New York, NY 10036. All entries must be received by Bantam Doubleday Dell postmarked no later than December 19, 1997. No mechanically reproduced entries allowed. Not responsible for lost, late, damaged, misdirected, or postage-due mail. By entering the sweepstakes, each entrant agrees to be bound by these rules and the decision of the judges, which shall be final and binding. Limit one entry per person.

The sweepstakes is open to children between the ages of 8 and 15 years of age (as of July 15, 1997), who are residents of the United States and Canada, excluding the Province of Quebec. The winner, if Canadian, will be required to answer correctly a time-limited arithmetic skill question in order to receive the prize. Employees of Bantam Doubleday Dell Publishing Group, Inc., and its subsidiaries and affiliates and their immediate family members are not eligible. Void where prohibited or restricted by law. Grand Prize will be awarded in the name of parent or legal guardian.

II. PRIZE

Grand Prize: Approximate Retail Value totals $1,000. Consists of:
• Apple eMate 300 mobile computer that can interact with both Mac®OS and Windows-based desktop units. The eMate comes with a pre-loaded software bundle and Web browser to provide access to the Internet.

III. WINNER

Winner will be chosen in a random drawing on or about January 2, 1998, from among all completed entry forms. Winner will be notified by mail. Odds of winning depend on the number of entries received. No substitution or transfer of the prize is allowed. All entries become the property of BDD and will not be returned. Taxes, if any, are the sole responsibility of the winner. BDD RESERVES THE RIGHT TO SUBSTITUTE A PRIZE OF EQUAL VALUE IF PRIZE, AS STATED ABOVE, BECOMES UNAVAILABLE. Winner and their legal guardian will be required to execute and return, within 14 days of notification, affidavit of eligibility and release. Noncompliance within this time period, or the return of any prize notification as undeliverable, will result in disqualification and the selection of an alternate winner. In the event of any other noncompliance with rules and conditions, prize may be awarded to an alternate winner. For a list of winners (available after January 31, 1998), send a self-addressed, stamped envelope entirely separate from your entry to: Bantam Doubleday Dell, Attn: Computer Winner, 1540 Broadway, 20th Floor, New York, NY 10036.